Forty Dead Men

Books by Donis Casey

The Alafair Tucker Mysteries
The Old Buzzard Had It Coming
Hornswoggled
The Drop Edge of Yonder
The Sky Took Him
Crying Blood
The Wrong Hill to Die On
Hell With The Lid Blown Off
All Men Fear Me
The Return of the Raven Mocker
Forty Dead Men

Forty Dead Men

An Alafair Tucker Mystery

Donis Casey

Poisoned Pen Press

First Edition 2018

10 9 8 7 6 5 4 3 2 1

Library of Congress Catalog Number: 2017946813

ISBN: 9781464209376   Hardcover
       9781464209390   Trade Paperback

Poisoned Pen Press
4014 N. Goldwater Boulevard, #201
Scottsdale, Arizona 85251
www.poisonedpenpress.com
info@poisonedpenpress.com

Printed in the United States of America

For my own personal veterans, with love.
Carl D. Casey, USMC 1942-1945, South Pacific
Larry Hull, USN, 1964-1969, Vietnam
Joseph R. Potter, USA, 1997-1999, 2001-2004, Iraq
Leah Irizarry, USA, 2007-2015, South Korea

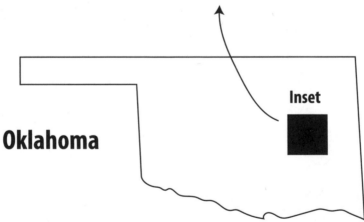

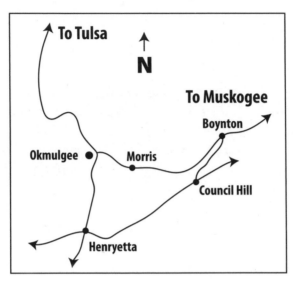

To Tulsa

N

To Muskogee

Boynton

Okmulgee   Morris

Council Hill

Henryetta

Inset

Oklahoma

Cast of Characters

Alafair Tucker—Mother of ten, who would do anything for her children

Shaw Tucker—Her husband, who would also do anything for his children

Their Children

Martha McCoy—age 27, and Major Streeter McCoy, her husband

Mary Lucas—age 26, and Sergeant Kurt Lucas, her husband
    Judy Lucas—age 3, their daughter

Alice Kelley—(Phoebe's twin) age 24, and Walter Kelley, her husband
    Linda Kelley—almost age 3, their daughter

Phoebe Day—(Alice's twin) age 24, and John Lee Day, her husband
    Zeltha Day—age 4, their daughter
    Tucker Day—age also not quite 3, their son
    George H. Day—age 6 weeks

Lieutenant George W. Tucker, known as Gee Dub, recently mustered out of the Army—age 22

Ruth Tucker—age 20, and Trenton Calder, her intended

Private Charlie Tucker—age 18

Blanche Tucker—age 13

Sophronia Tucker—age 12

Grace Tucker—age 6

Other Members of the Family
Chase Kemp—age 9, Alafair's nephew and ward

Scott Tucker—the law in Boynton, Oklahoma, Shaw's cousin

Charles Tucker—Shaw's brother

Lavinia Tucker—Charles' wife

Sally McBride—Shaw's mother

Peter McBride—Shaw's stepfather

Other Folks Who Must be Dealt With
Daniel Johnson—dead

Harvey Stump—also dead

Holly Thornberry Johnson—Daniel's widow

Pearl Evans Johnson—also Daniel's widow

Lucy Johnson—Daniel's mother

Fern Johnson—Daniel's father

Bertram Evans—Pearl's father

Leon Stryker—Pearl's fiancé

Private Richard J. Moretti—from Gee Dub's unit in France

Lieutenant Nigel Anderson—a British officer

Sharma—Anderson's batman

Abner Meriwether—the lawyer

Amos Gundry—the U.S. Marshal

Granny Murray—saw what happened

Joan McNamara—heard things

Chief Bowman—Chief of Okmulgee Police Department

Critters
Penny—Gee Dub's chestnut mare

Charlie Dog, Bacon, Buttercup, Crook—the family dogs

Various cats, a goat, and Gregory the Duck

Chapter One

Scott Tucker, constable for the town of Boynton, Oklahoma, was glad to have his deputy back. His eldest son, Slim Tucker, had made an adequate fill-in deputy while Trenton Calder was away on a ship in the North Atlantic, fighting the War to End All Wars, but Slim was an oilman down to his toes, and though he had done his duty to his father, his heart hadn't been in it. Slim was now back surveying for the Pure Oil Company, where he belonged, and Trent had donned his badge again.

The only problem was that Trent wasn't going to last. Trent had been content to work for Scott for little more than room and board and pocket money when he was innocent and footloose and barely out of his teens. But now Trent was twenty-four years old, had seen the world, and was soon to be married to Scott's young cousin once-removed, Ruth Tucker. As soon as Trent returned to work, he had informed Scott that the arrangement was only temporary, just until he could find a job that would actually support himself and a wife. Or until Scott could find another adventuresome youngster who was too dumb to know better than to take on the job.

Trent had always been a serious young man, and that had certainly not changed after his stint in the Navy. In fact, he was even more inclined to keep his own counsel since his return.

Scott knew better than to ask him what had happened to him while he was at sea. Trent didn't volunteer any information. He only said that if he never again saw a body of water bigger than a farm pond, that would suit him just fine.

Scott knew that he was not going to find an experienced replacement deputy—he was going to have to find a green boy and raise him himself, like he had done with Trent. The thought made him tired. In fact, ever since he had gotten over the bout of Spanish flu that had afflicted him the previous fall, Scott didn't much have the energy for anything. Over the past few months, he had been thinking of telling the town council that they should start looking for someone else to keep the peace in Boynton. Perhaps the town had become big enough to hire a marshal, or request that the county assign a real deputy sheriff to the area.

He was sitting at his desk in the jailhouse on a fine December morning, pondering that very notion, when Trent came in from his rounds.

"Clelland Rogers and his wife found a dead soldier," Trent said, without even a how-do-you-do.

Scott looked up, startled. "What's this?"

Trent hooked his thumbs in his belt and shifted his weight to one foot. "They was driving in from Muskogee when Clel felt the call of nature and went off behind a tree about a mile and a half east of town. He says he seen a boot sticking out from behind a bush and went over to investigate. That's when he found him. Still in his uniform and all. Mindy tells me Clel thinks the soldier has been dead for a spell."

Scott had stood and was retrieving his gun belt from his top desk drawer. "Where is Clel now?"

"He's still out there. Mindy came on into town to let us know. Clel stayed out there so we could find the place again."

They spotted Clel sitting on a stump by the side of the road some distance east of town. He stood up when he saw the auto approaching and moseyed out to meet them with a smile. Finding a dead body didn't seem to have spoiled his day. But that was Clel. Scott had known Clel Rogers all his life—a tall, good-natured man, untroubled by deep thought. He had taken over his father's furniture store when Clel Senior retired, and had married a local girl a few months earlier. He was an innocuous fellow, and an honest-enough businessman, with thinning blond hair, a round face and jug ears, and the pasty complexion of a man who spends too much of his time indoors. How he had convinced a pretty girl like Mindy to marry him was something of a puzzle to Scott.

Clel pointed to the shrubbery several feet back from the road. "Body's over yonder."

They followed him through the tall grass to a clump of sumac bushes on the side of a little hill. They could smell the soldier before they could see him, so Scott was relieved to see that the body was still in fair shape. The face was blue-tinged, and the soldier had suffered a bout of vomiting and diarrhea before he met his maker. Scott figured he was probably walking along the road when the influenza overcame him and he crawled off into the grass to be sick. The influenza epidemic that year had already killed millions around the world.

He turned to Trent. "Son, go to the car and bring me that blanket to cover him up." Scott was not worried about infection since he had recently recovered from the flu himself. But he was not happy about having to go through the man's pockets. There was not much in them. No money, no bag that they could find. He did have a military ID in the front breast pocket of his tunic, and a worn identity disc in a trouser pocket.

The photo in the ID was of a bemused-looking young man whose new military haircut left him practically bald, except for a dark topknot that stuck straight up, as though he had poked a finger in an electric light socket. His home address was in Okmulgee. Scott sighed. The poor son-of-a-gun had made it through the war, only to die of the flu eighteen miles from home.

Chapter Two

Alafair Tucker finally found the time to do some cleaning in the bunk room at the back of the toolshed. Mop the floor, dust, pick up the dirty laundry off the floor, make the bed. She didn't know where Gee Dub was. He didn't bother to keep anyone apprised of his whereabouts these days. Certainly not his mother. Of course, he had just been discharged from the Army and only been home for less than a week. He had not had time to settle into a routine. When he first stepped off the train at the Boynton station, he had made it plain to his folks that he could use a few days to rest and do nothing before deciding what to do with the rest of his life. He had been studying agriculture at Oklahoma A&M before the war started and he volunteered for the Army before he could be drafted. But he had told his parents that after his year in Europe, he was not at all sure he would be able to pick up where he left off, as though nothing had happened.

Of course, if Gee Dub did decide to work the family farm again, helping raise and train horses and mules, his father would have to pay him. Gee Dub was twenty-two years old. He'd gone to Europe to fight the Hun. He could no longer be expected to be one of Shaw Tucker's unpaid child labor force.

Gee Dub had changed. No one other than Alafair seemed to be aware of it, but she knew it was true. To everyone else, friends and family alike, Gee Dub was still the quiet, sharp-eyed, good-natured young man with the wry sense of humor that he had been before he shipped out for France. His siblings thought he was the same, and even Shaw told Alafair that he couldn't see what she was talking about. But Alafair knew.

The entire family had been waiting for him when his train arrived at the Boynton station on Monday-before-last. "Where's Gee? Where's Gee?" Grace kept asking, as several people disembarked—a well-fed couple verging on elderly, a young lady. A soldier caused a momentary stir, until they recognized him as Johnny Turner, son of the owner of the livery stable.

"Gee Dub's right behind me," Johnny called to the Tuckers with a wave, before his own mother and father enveloped him and swept him away.

Then a second man in uniform stepped down onto the platform. He was tall and dark like Gee Dub, and had a peculiar twisty smile like Gee Dub's, too. But Alafair was taken aback when all the siblings rushed at this unknown soldier. He looked like Gee Dub, but there was something so different about his eyes that she hadn't recognized him. Her own firstborn son.

"Hello, Mama," he had said, and Alafair had finally seen him with her heart. Yes, he was hers, but he was not entirely the same young man who had left Boynton for Fort Reilly from this very station in 1917.

It was true that he didn't behave differently. He laughed and played with the grandchildren and the dogs and teased his sisters. He ate like there was no tomorrow. He sat with the family after supper and sang and played his guitar and told stories, as he always had done. He took up residence in the toolshed bunk room behind the barn, just where he had been living before he left for basic training. But sometimes a faraway look would come over his face and, even though his body was still there, Alafair saw that his soul was somewhere else. Every day since his return, he would saddle his chestnut mare, Penny, after dinner and disappear until suppertime. He never said where he was going. Alafair thought he probably didn't know himself. He didn't go to town, or Alafair would have heard from someone who had seen him. Shaw told her he more than likely rode into the country to be alone and get himself oriented to civilian life again.

Alafair had scrubbed and prettified the bunk room behind the barn to a fare-thee-well when she first knew that he was coming home for good, but until today she had not had a minute to clean since he had taken up residence. Her middle daughter, Ruth, was to be married in a few weeks now that her betrothed, Cousin Scott Tucker's red-haired deputy Trenton Calder, was home from the Navy, and Alafair had been spending most of her rare free moments sewing on a trousseau.

But it had been nearly a week since she had cleaned up after Gee Dub, and she couldn't put it off any longer. She had no idea what his stint in the Army had done for Gee Dub's housekeeping skills. He had spent the bulk of his time overseas living in a muddy trench, which had probably increased his tolerance for dirt.

Alafair's fourth daughter, Phoebe, was visiting today with her three little children. Phoebe's youngest, George H. Day, had been born only six weeks earlier and was a source of endless amusement and fascination to his older siblings, Zeltha and Tuck. No one ever called the baby anything other than George H., which may have been a pretty fancy handle for such a wiggly little tadpole, but the extended Tucker family boasted so many Georges that this new generation of parents had to scramble to come up with ways to designate which one belonged to whom.

Dinner was over and the men had gone back to work. Alafair was on the back porch washing out a couple of diapers when she saw Gee Dub ride off toward the woods. She wrung out the diaper she was holding and hung it over a line strung across the porch before hurrying back into the house to retrieve her mop, bucket, rags, and a set of fresh sheets. After directing Grace, her six-year-old, to help with the little ones, she left Phoebe and the children in the kitchen giving George H. his dinner, and headed out to the bunk room.

She had no compunction about invading Gee Dub's privacy. She had always cleaned the bunk room, no matter who was living

there, and Gee Dub was certainly aware of that. If he had something to hide, he would have taken up residence somewhere else.

• • ● • •

The bedroom that had been carved out of part of Shaw's toolshed was basic, but comfortable. The furniture was recycled
and threadbare, yet serviceable. The two iron bedsteads sported
relatively new horsehair mattresses, tufted to hold the filling in
place and the edges hand-stitched together. A painted wooden
table with two chairs sat in the center of the room. A washstand
with a pitcher and chipped basin, small chest of drawers, and a
Franklin stove in one corner completed the furnishings. The one
window on the back wall was covered by curtains that Alafair
had made from two of her old calico aprons.

She leaned over to strip the sheets off the bed Gee Dub had
been using, and hesitated when she saw that he had placed two
small yellow boxes under his pillow. Rifle cartridges. She blinked
at the boxes before she picked them up. One box was empty,
and the weight and forlorn rattle within told her that the other
was nearly so. She sat down on the edge of the bed and slid the
box open to find one cartridge.

One bullet left.

On Gee Dub's eighteenth birthday, his father had given him
his own Springfield rifle. Gee Dub loved that firearm, and it had
broken his heart when he was forced to leave it at home when
he went to the Army. The boxes under the pillow were U.S.
Army-issue, once containing twenty cartridges each, .30-06
Springfield, steel-tipped. Gee Dub's own rifle used the same
type of ammunition.

Alafair regarded the solitary remaining cartridge for some
minutes, mulling over the possibilities. Why would Gee Dub
keep two practically empty boxes for military ammunition
under his pillow? Did he sleep on them? It wouldn't be a very
comfortable arrangement if he did. The empty boxes must mean
something to him, and Alafair did not like to think about what

that could be. He had been a riflery instructor at Camp Funston in Kansas for the first six months after his OCS training before he had been shipped off to France with his unit, where he had been in command of his own frontline platoon. The family knew that he and his men had been in the trenches for a few months, but then Gee Dub had been pulled off the line and assigned to a British unit to carry out some sort of special detail. He had just been transferred back to the Americans when the war ended. He had spent only a few more weeks in France before he was sent back to the States to be mustered out. She didn't know the particulars of his service. He had never said.

He had never said very much at all about his time in France. That did not surprise anyone. Gee Dub had never been a big talker.

Alafair wondered, but she knew she would not ask her son what significance the boxes held for him. If he wanted her to know, he would tell her. She changed the sheets and pillow case, shook out the blankets, and replaced the boxes where she had found them. She would mention her find to Shaw tonight, after they had gone to bed. Not that she expected him to do anything, but sometimes it's important to share your burdens.

Chapter Three

Gee Dub dismounted and sat down on the knoll with his rifle across his lap. The isolated hill was one of his favorite places in the world. It was located just at the edge of the woods, overlooking the south-facing bank on a bend of Cloud Creek, which was running high this February after the winter rains. The dappled shade of the pin oaks provided camouflage, so it would be hard for the odd casual passerby to see him. But he could see out across the fields to the north for some miles. The silence and solitude comforted him. After the continual clamor and horror of the front, he had lost his tolerance for most any kind of noise. Since he had come home, he had ridden out here every day to spend hours on his own in the quiet peace of nature and wait for his thinking processes to start up again.

He had been unable to plan more than ten minutes into the future for some months. Or to plan at all, really. Since France, he could only react to whatever circumstance he found himself in.

He removed a blanket roll from behind his saddle and unfurled it on the ground before seating himself on it. He sat for a moment, enjoying the luxury of the blanket between his behind and the dry yellow grass. After weeks in a filthy, muddy ditch he appreciated small comforts more than he used to. February was drawing to a close, and the air was distinctly chilly. The leaves still clinging to the branches of the pin oaks had turned brown, and he found their continual wind-driven papery susurration soothing as he stared blankly across the empty fields on the other side of the creek.

He had spent the first twenty years of his life on his parents' farm. He had never lived anywhere else. But after spending just a few months in France, everything he had ever known had changed. The morning he had stepped down off the train at the Boynton station was seared in his memory. His younger sisters had halfway grown up. He almost didn't recognize the youngest, Grace. He certainly wouldn't have known his infant nieces and nephews if he had had to pick them out of a crowd. And they didn't know him from Adam, either. A year and a half is a long time in the life of a two-year-old. His older sisters looked the same, though—beautiful butterflies, teasing, warm, and doting. In the space of half a minute he went from ecstatic joy and affection, to grief at what he had missed, to blank nothingness. Seeing his parents gave him a jolt. It was as though he had never really looked at them before that day. His mother surprised him the most. He didn't remember how small she was. It was odd. She had always loomed so large in his life.

He had been home a week, but he was still disjointed, riding the waves between emotion and the void.

How long he sat there, he could not tell. He might have fallen asleep, though he didn't remember doing so. He came to with a start and looked at the sky. He had been in that strange state in which time passed without involving him. The sun had moved a hand-span. A little more than an hour. He was not surprised. But then he would not have been surprised if the entire day had passed. Or only a few minutes.

A noise behind him caused him to start. He twisted around on the blanket to see a thin young man in an Army uniform standing at the edge of the woods. The man yelped and threw up his hands. "Hang on there, Lieutenant, it's only me!"

Gee Dub blinked, still not quite returned from wherever he had been. It dawned on him that his revolver was clutched in his right hand and aimed squarely at a spot between the young man's eyes. "Moretti?"

"Yessir, it's me. You think you could lower that pistol?"

Gee Dub let his arm sink to his side. "Moretti? What in the…what are you doing here? I thought you got sent home to Pennsylvania."

"I did, Lieutenant. But, hey, I felt an itch to see you again. Besides, I got no use for the slate mines anymore."

"How in the name of Pete did you know where to find me?"

"It wasn't hard. You told us all enough about Boynton and your folks' farm. I'd have looked for you at the house, but I caught sight of you sitting up here on this hill. I just didn't know what to do with myself after France, so I took a wild hair and came down to Oklahoma to look up my old commander. I wanted to see what became of you."

"You never were all that smart, I reckon. You got somewhere to stay, Moretti?"

"I just got here, Lieutenant."

Gee Dub fell silent and studied the young man's face for a minute or two. A small, thin little guy, so young, with black hair and dancing brown eyes. He had never expected to see Private Moretti again, and to have him turn up out of the blue like this was hard to accept. In fact he could hardly believe his own eyes. He wondered if he looked as stunned as he felt. "Moretti," he murmured, and the young man smiled.

"Yes, sir."

Gee Dub shook himself and stood up. "Well, I have an extra cot in my room behind the barn. You're welcome to bunk with me while you're here. And quit calling me Lieutenant. You might as well call me Gee Dub, like everybody else around here. I ain't your superior officer anymore."

"Oh, I don't think I could do that, Mr. Tucker. It's too late for me to change now. You can call me Dickie, though."

"I'm not going to call you Dickie, Moretti. That's a stupid name for a grown up man. How about Dick. Or Rick, or Richard?"

"I wouldn't know who those guys are, Mr. Tucker. I been Dickie all my life."

"I reckon I'll have to keep calling you Moretti, then. Come on up to the house and meet my folks. It's about dinner time anyway."

"Thanks, but I'm pooped. If you don't mind us going back to your room now, I think I'll just have a little nap. Maybe later I'll head to town and look around. I've never been to Oklahoma, you know."

"Suit yourself."

• • ● • •

Gee Dub left Moretti stretched out on his extra cot and made his way up to the house for supper. Shaw had come in from the fields and was already seated at his accustomed place at the head of the huge oak table in the kitchen. Alafair was at the cookstove, ladling food out of pots and into bowls, while Gee Dub's three youngest sisters, thirteen-year-old Blanche; Sophronia, age twelve; and six-year-old Grace, were ferrying serving dishes from the stove to the table. Phoebe and her children were still there, joined by Phoebe's husband, John Lee Day, whose gimpy leg and bad eye had prevented him from going into the service. Gee Dub made his greetings properly and sat down in the empty chair between John Lee and Phoebe, who was holding her newborn in her lap.

"I expect I'd better lend Mama a hand," Phoebe said. She stood up and thrust the baby at Gee Dub. "Here. Hold on to George H. for a spell."

Gee Dub was no stranger to holding newborn babies, but it had been a while. Last time was the little fellow he had dug out of the rubble of that bombed house in Château-Thierry. That one had been a little older than this tad. George H. was staring up at him with a speculative expression, not yet willing to decide what he thought of this newfound uncle.

"His name is George H."

Gee Dub looked down at the owner of the high-pitched voice who had just spoken. Zeltha Day was standing by his left leg. Phoebe's oldest had been not much more than a toddler when he left. She was a big-eyed four-year-old now. "I know it," he said.

Zeltha had one hand on John Lee's thigh as she gazed up at her uncle. "Mama says you're her brother. You've been away at the war."

"That's right."

"George H. is my brother," she informed him. "I was hoping for a sister. Tuck is enough brother for anybody. But Mama said we don't get to choose what kind of baby we get."

Gee Dub gave the baby a critical once-over. "He doesn't look like much trouble."

She shrugged. "He's all right, I guess. He don't do much."

"You'll have to raise him to suit you. You want to hold him?"

She lifted her hand off her father's leg and gestured no. "Mama don't let me hold him yet."

"What does your mama let you do?"

"I like to play with my animals. I like all animals. I got a white cat that lives in the barn, and a baby goat, and a duck."

Gee Dub shifted George H. to the other arm and winked at Zeltha's doting father before he replied. "What're their names, these animals?"

"The cat don't have a name. I call the goat Goatie. The duck is named Gregory."

Gee Dub lifted an eyebrow. "Gregory? That's right fancy for a duck."

"Fronie won't call him by his right name. She calls him Ducky-Doodle." Zeltha was insulted by the slight.

Behind him, Gee Dub heard his sister Sophronia bark out a laugh, and a chuckle escaped him before he could catch it. "She's just teasing you. I'm sure Gregory is fine specimen of duckhood."

"I love him." Zeltha's expression attested to her sincerity. "I even taught him to do a trick."

"A trick!"

"When I say 'flap,' he flaps his wings like this." She demonstrated.

"Well, that's amazing. You can show me next time I'm over to your place. Why doesn't your cat have a name?"

Zeltha moved closer and draped her arms over his knee, the better to carry on an intimate conversation. "He wouldn't know his name to hear it. Mama says white cats are deaf."

"I've heard that. Cats don't generally come when you call them, anyway."

Zeltha gave a philosophical nod. "That's true."

George H. started to fuss and Gee Dub began to bounce him in his arms.

"He's probably wet," Zeltha said.

Gee Dub put a hand on the back of the baby's neck and maneuvered him into a saggy sitting position on his knee. "He is, indeed. You know where your grandma has stowed his drawers?"

She nodded vigorously.

"Run fetch one."

Zeltha streaked out of the kitchen and Phoebe held out her arms. "Give him here, Gee, before you get stuck with diaper-duty."

As Phoebe left the room with her damp baby, Sophronia turned from her task to shoot Gee Dub an amused glance. "You're a pretty good hand with children."

"I had a lot of practice with the rest of you lot."

John Lee laughed. "You ought to get some of your own. I guarantee they'll keep you on your toes."

Gee Dub snorted. "Y'all quit trying to marry me off. When I get the notion, I'll manage that task on my own."

• ● ● ● •

Supper consisted of leftovers from the larger midday meal, but there was still plenty of food, and Gee Dub indulged himself to the full. After eighteen months of Army rations, he had developed a rare appreciation for his mother's home cooking. Besides, he suspected that Alafair was making a point of cooking his favorite dishes as a homecoming treat, and he intended to make the most of it while it lasted. He had not told her that he had taken to hoarding leftovers in his room—anything easily portable that he could sneak out of the house. He had even spirited away a couple of mason jars of home-canned fruit and green tomato relish from her pantry. He was aware that this was an odd thing to do. His mother would have cheerfully let him take anything he wanted.

After supper was over, the men repaired to the parlor for a few minutes of farm talk before the women finished cleanup and joined them. Gee Dub retrieved a guitar from his parents' bedroom and began to noodle out a quiet tune from his seat next to the piano. Alafair came in from the kitchen and sat down in her armchair with her mending in her lap. Tuck was playing with the family's long-legged mutt, Bacon, on a rag rug beside Alafair's chair. The other family pet, Bacon's daddy, Charlie Dog, snored softly by Shaw's feet. In the way of all two-and-a-half-year-olds, Tuck suddenly got an idea in his head and jumped up off the floor, startling the dog, and ran over to Shaw. He clambered up into Shaw's lap and placed his hands on either side of his grandfather's face. Apparently, Tuck had come up with a delightful idea, because his words tumbled out so fast that it was hard to understand what he was saying.

"Flabber me, Grampa!" he cried, and Shaw lifted the toddler's shirt to blow a raspberry against the boy's tummy, eliciting peals of laughter. Alafair and the girls began to laugh as well, because who can resist a little child's hilarity?

Gee Dub did not laugh. He was disoriented, as though he had just awakened from a dream. Why was Tuck still here? Phoebe and John Lee had gone home. They must have left Tuck to spend the night with the grandparents. There was always some grandchild here. At least one, maybe two or three, seldom the same combination. Somebody sitting on a pile of pillows in a kitchen chair, a little pair of eyes peeping over the edge of the table at supper. A roly-poly form sleeping on a pallet on the floor of Granma and Grampa's bedroom with her thumb stuck in her mouth and long eyelashes curving over her apple-red cheeks.

Gee Dub was suddenly hyper-aware. Alafair stopped laughing long enough to stick the end of a long strand of black thread into her mouth. She drew it out, twirled the end between her thumb and forefinger, and threaded a needle by feel. Gee Dub watched the deft movement of her fingers. How did she manage to poke that cotton thread through the infinitesimally small eye of the needle without even looking at her hands?

Gee Dub stood up and walked out of the parlor, through the kitchen, and onto the back porch. He expected that the family was too busy being entertained by Tuck to notice that he had left.

• • ● • •

When Gee Dub got back to the bunk room, Moretti was sitting at the table. He had ditched the uniform and was dressed in regular civvies. "Where you been all evening?" Gee Dub asked him.

"Looking around. Yourself?"

Gee Dub took off his hat and hung it on a peg beside the door before sitting down on the side of his bunk. "Up to the house. My sister and brother-in-law came to supper with their three little rascals in tow."

"You're in a pretty good mood, Lieutenant. You must have enjoyed the little imps."

He shrugged, then acquiesced with a nod. "I played my guitar for a while, and music always cheers me up. Besides, it's always a hoot to play with the youngsters. How 'bout you, Private? What did you think of Boynton?"

"Well, it's no Pittsburgh, but it'll do." He stood and stretched. "Well, I'm going to bed. It's been a long day. Hard to know what to do with myself. It's going to take me longer than I thought to get used to civilian life again."

"It's strange when nobody is shooting at you," Gee Dub said.

"Maybe that's it."

Gee Dub skinned off his shirt and trousers, blew out the lamp, and lay back on his bunk. The ceiling had been recently whitewashed. Funny, he hadn't noticed that before tonight. Whitewash couldn't cover the cracks and weathering in the boards. The room had been carved out of one end of the old toolshed that Shaw had built by hand over twenty years earlier. This shed was older than the house. *Can't make a silk purse out of a sow's ear*, he thought. He was just drifting off to sleep when it occurred to him that he had never mentioned Moretti to his family.

Chapter Four

The next morning, the bed that Gee Dub had made up for Moretti was empty and Army-neat. Gee Dub figured his guest had gone back into town and he wouldn't see him for the rest of the day. He'd wait until this evening to introduce Private Moretti to his folks. He dressed quickly and stepped outside.

The weather had changed. It was late February in Oklahoma, so there was no telling what any particular day would be like, or even any hour. Yesterday had been quiet and sunny, but a front had moved in overnight, and it was cold, cloudy, and spitting icy little needles of rain.

He heard a loud chirp, a rustle and flutter, and was just turning toward the sound when he was startled by a flash of gray feathers. He groped for his sidearm, but it wasn't there. Just as well. Another swoop and he saw that he was being dive-bombed by an incensed mockingbird bent on giving him a warning. He took a breath to try and calm his heart. He recognized the behavior. Winter was having its last hurrah, but spring was near and the mockingbird was building a nest somewhere at hand. He moved far enough from the door to placate the bird and watched her disappear under the eaves of the toolshed. He could barely make out a corner of the nest under the shelter of the roof. The mother bird did not dive at him again, but settled on the edge of the roof and chittered at him. *Keep your distance.*

"Tell you what, Mother," he called, "let's call a truce. You don't bother me and I won't let anybody bother you."

She cocked her head and gave him a calculating look with one bright black eye, then disappeared under the eaves.

Gee Dub stood outside the door for a minute and studied the sky with detached interest while the freezing rain numbed his cheeks. It was uncomfortable. It was downright painful, which gave Gee Dub a perverse pleasure. He pulled his hat down far enough to protect the skin on his face before the cold could do him some damage. While he didn't much care about his face, he did care about his fingers. He had had frostbitten toes before, and it had taken him a while to recover enough to walk without clumping along like an elephant. He didn't mind the pain, but he did mind not being able to get out of the way if he needed to, and it was important that he not lose his ability to squeeze a trigger.

He made his way to the barn and saddled his mare. After spending yesterday evening with his family, he had had all the domestic comfort he could tolerate for the moment. Penny was not happy to leave the relative warmth of the barn, but after a snort and a head-toss, she did her duty and carried him across the fields and up to his hill.

He dismounted and rolled out his blanket, allowing Penny to graze on her own. The cold wind was gusty. Gee Dub had always been prone to earaches, and cold wind was the worst. The temperature alone had already affected his hearing. He knew from experience that an hour in frigid wind meant he would be spending the next week with an agonizing earache. He had a sudden flashback to his mother dropping warm oil into his sore ear, then pressing a heated towel-wrapped saucer to the side of his head.

The memory of his mother comforting him, of taking care of him, of trying to relieve his pain, horrified him, stabbed him like a knife. He wrapped his knitted scarf around his ears, leaving only his eyes uncovered. He was going to have to take care not to get sick while he was here. At least not sick enough for his mother to notice.

It dawned on him that he had been away for awhile, lost in his own thoughts. Something had changed about the scene. He was looking at a person, striding purposefully up the road with a carpetbag in hand. A woman. He was surprised to see her, or to see anyone at all. The road was not really a road at all. It was more of a path, two ruts in the landscape, flattened by repeated passes of Shaw's hay wagon.

The woman appeared to know where she was going. At least she gave that impression until she reached the middle of the field. Gee Dub watched as her step faltered. She hesitated, set her bag down on the grass and sat herself on top of it, her back to the wind. She seemed small. Or perhaps it was the distance. She clasped her arms around herself and hunched over, trying to protect herself from the rain. Her posture made her look miserable, and lost.

Gee Dub stood up and walked back toward Penny, who had sensibly withdrawn into the woods a few yards behind him. He seized her reins and lifted himself into the saddle. It took a while for him to reach the lost woman on the other side of the creek. He had to backtrack through the woods to the farm road about a half-mile west. He rode to the footbridge that crossed Cloud Creek, then down to the wagon track where the woman was sitting in the field. He had expected that she would be long gone by the time he made his way around the creek, but when he reached the wagon track he could still see her forlorn figure, sitting on her carpet bag in the middle of a rut.

When he turned the horse down the track, the woman raised her head and watched him come toward her. She did not stand until he reined in. The two of them took one another's measure for a few seconds, as well as they could do, considering that both of them were wrapped to the gills, hatted, scarfed, coated to a fare-thee-well.

She was a small woman, Gee Dub had been right about that. Her age was a mystery, her face covered as it was, but Gee Dub deduced from the high arch of her brows and the width of her striking amber eyes that she was young enough.

"You lost?" he said.

She didn't reply. She took a step backwards and stumbled over her bag. He couldn't judge her expression, but her posture was stiff. A tall, unknown man on horseback looming over her out in the middle of nowhere had to be frightening.

His voice softened. "Don't worry, Miss. I don't mean you no harm. The name is George W. Tucker. This is my family's farm that you're walking across. I saw you from atop that hill yonder, on the other side of the creek. You seem to be taking a cold and unpleasant hike to nowhere. Can I provide you with some direction?"

The woman seemed marginally relieved at his civilized manner. "I'm sorry if I'm trespassing. I was walking on the main road, but a passerby told me that this track was a shorter route to Boynton." Her low-pitched, throaty voice was muffled by the woolen neck scarf that she had wrapped around her nose and mouth, but he could hear her timbre well enough to confirm that she was indeed young. She had an accent that he couldn't identify.

"Well, Miss, if you're coming from Muskogee, this track does cut a mile or so off the trip. But you've about two miles to town yet, and this is mighty foul weather for a stroll."

"I don't have money for a conveyance," she said, too quickly. "I don't have anything of value. If you'll just point me in the right direction, I'll be on my way."

Her fear clutched at his heart. He had been about to offer her a ride. Gee Dub considered dismounting to be more on her level, but decided that she would be less alarmed if he didn't make any untoward moves. He sidled Penny away from her a few steps, giving her some space. "You're heading in the right direction. Just keep to this track for another quarter-mile. You'll come to a barbed-wire fence, but there's a stile to the side of the path. Once you're over it, you'll be on a better road. Head south…that way…another couple miles. Stick to the road and you can't get lost."

The woman picked up her bag and held it in front of herself like a shield. "Thank you."

"You sure I can't…?"

"I'm fine, Mister. You just go on your way and I'll go on mine."

He hesitated, half-expecting her to run away, but she stood her ground, waiting for him to leave before she felt safe enough to turn her back on him.

"All right, then." He touched his fingers to his hat brim in a salute. "I'll leave you to it. Best of luck to you, Miss."

He turned Penny's head and took out across the field at a canter. He purposely rode off in the opposite direction from the one he had told her to follow. He did not look around until he had reached the woods, but when he did he could see that she had not moved. She was watching him, wary, making sure that he was really leaving.

He guided his horse to a place where he could ford the stream, and headed directly back to the house. He threw Penny's reins over the post beside the back porch and went inside. Alafair was standing at the oak table in the middle of the kitchen, peeling potatoes. The big cast-iron cookstove was going full blast, warming the kitchen enough that Gee Dub's shoulders relaxed.

Alafair looked up from her paring and cocked an eyebrow. "What's up, son?"

• • ● • •

Once the tall stranger on the tall horse was well gone, the lost woman picked up her bag and walked briskly on in the rain. The fence appeared just where the cowboy had said it would. The woman crossed the stile, and half an hour later, she was trudging down the road when a buggy with the hood up against the rain came up behind her. She moved off to the side of the road, but the buggy came to a halt and a dark-eyed woman in a floppy-brimmed hat stuck her head around the hood.

"You shouldn't be walking in this rain, honey. You'll catch your death. Where you headed?"

The traveler raised a hand to keep the rain out of her eyes and gave her would-be rescuer the once-over. She was middle-aged and middle-sized at best, wrapped in a heavy cloth coat, sitting next to a young girl with curious black eyes and thick black braids.

"I'm trying to get to the next town. Are you going that way, ma'am?"

"You're going to Boynton? Climb on in." She handed the lost woman up and settled her next to the little girl. "I declare, you're about drowned! I'm Miz Tucker. This here is Grace."

"Howdy," Grace chirped.

The lost woman sank back in the upholstered seat, relieved to be out of the rain. "My name is Holly Johnson."

Alafair snapped the reins and the horse began to move. "Holly! What a pretty name. I never met a Holly. You look like you've been on the road a while, Holly. Are you looking to meet up with somebody in Boynton?"

"No, it's just the next town on the road to Okmulgee. But I want to get out of the weather and maybe have a rest. I've been walking all day and I'm bone-tired."

"When was the last time you ate?"

Holly didn't answer, but the question elicited an ironic laugh.

There was a moment of concerned silence before Alafair said, "Why don't you come back to the house with us and have a bite of dinner, Miz Johnson? Dry off and rest your feet for a spell. Once you're feeling better, I'll carry you on in to Boynton and drop you off wherever you want."

Holly's first inclination was to refuse, but it had been such a long journey, and so hard. She had felt like a fawn among jackals for so long that it was hard for her to trust anyone. The idea of warmth and food and kindness was so overwhelming that she had to brace herself sternly to keep from bursting into tears.

Alafair sensed her mood. "The house is just over yonder, less than a mile, honey. You've come this far, you might as well finish the journey a couple of hours later, rested and with a full belly."

• ● ⬤ ● •

Now that the hood of the buggy offered her some protection from the rain, Holly was able to take in the scenery. Since she had left Muskogee, the best she had been able to do was keep her eyes on her feet, to keep the rain out of her face and her shoes out of puddles. It was a misty, gray day, but the landscape was rather pleasant. The country was wide open, punctuated by rolling hills and large stands of native trees between cultivated fields that lay fallow this time of year. On the trip between Chicago and St. Louis, she had spent hours watching out the window as the train passed mile after mile of half-grown fields of winter wheat. After she reached Springfield, Missouri, the country had become one forested mountain after another. There was not much wheat here in eastern Oklahoma. She idly wondered what the farmers raised in these now-sodden black fields.

Mrs. Tucker steered the buggy off the main road and onto a well-graded section-line road that passed by a couple of neat farmhouses, a small herd of white-faced cattle, all facing in the same direction, rear ends to the rain, and endless stretches of barbed-wire fence.

The gray mare pulling the buggy lifted her head and picked up the pace of her own volition, so Holly expected that they were nearing Mrs. Tucker's house. She was proved right when they pulled up in front of a wide wooden gate and the little girl jumped down without a word to swing it open and allow the buggy to drive through. Mrs. Tucker pulled up long enough to let Grace close the gate behind them and climb back up beside Holly. Grace gave Holly a grin of accomplishment. Her two top baby teeth had made their exit and one white incisor was just beginning to erupt. Holly grinned back, charmed in spite of herself.

She could see the house in the distance. It was a typical country farmhouse, a white clapboard square with a long covered porch running across the front. A white picket fence surrounded the yard, and an old-fashioned stone well with a wooden cap over the opening stood in one corner. An enormous garden took up one entire side of the yard and spilled over onto the adjacent plot of land. To Holly's surprise, close to the house a few vegetables had already poked up through the soil. She could identify a couple of varieties of lettuce, some onion tops, and radish leaves. Where she came from, it was far too early to think about starting a truck garden.

Alafair drove to the back of the house and halted in front of a ringed hitching post beside the back door. They entered the house through the screened-in back porch, which was alive with potted plants and fragrant with drying herbs hanging from the rafters. A clothesline, draped with drying shirts, had been strung across one corner of the porch.

Grace ran ahead and Alafair steered Holly into the kitchen after her. Holly took a long minute to get herself oriented. The kitchen was dominated by a cast-iron cookstove almost as big as the buggy they had driven in on. Two girls on the verge of adolescence—one tall dark-haired beauty with striking green eyes and one small wraith with frizzy reddish hair and a wealth of freckles—were standing in the middle of the floor eyeing her with unabashed curiosity.

Alalfair waved toward them. "Miz Johnson, these are some more of my girls. That one is Blanche and that's Sophronia."

"Call me Fronie, Miz Johnson," the freckle-face said. "Everybody else does."

Alafair took charge. "Fronie, run out and take care of Missy and the buggy for me. Miz Johnson, take off them wet things and hang them over there on that hat tree beside the stove. They'll be dry by the time dinner's over. Have a seat yonder. Grace, get our guest a plate and utensils. Miz Johnson, honey, would you like coffee or tea? Now, you need to drink something hot with lots of sugar, warm up your innards. Blanche, pour our guest a mug of coffee."

Holly sat numbly at the end of the table while the girls fussed around her. A dog, an aged yellow shepherd, ambled into the kitchen, plopped down beside her chair, and leaned his substantial bulk against her leg.

"That's Charlie Dog," Grace said. "He likes you."

The old dog shifted to lie across Holly's feet under the table. His warmth was comforting. Holly smiled. "I like him, too."

Alafair went out the back door, and Holly heard her calling, a meaningless high-register holler that surely carried for miles—*Oooo-eee.*

Holly did not understand what Alafair was doing. She didn't understand much these days. This country, this life, was far removed from her experience. But she was at the end of her endurance, and had no strength left to make sense of anything.

Alafair came back inside as though nothing unusual had just occurred, and took up a post at the stove to ladle soupy green beans and fatback out of a pot and into a serving dish. The girls piled dish after dish of vegetables onto the table, as well as an enormous platter of fried pork. When Holly was convinced that there was no room left on the table for one more saucer, she heard the sound of boots on the porch and men's voices. The girls flitted around the table and settled into their seats like a flock of birds settling on a wire.

The back door opened and two men entered. Obviously father and son. Both black-haired, with high cheekbones and almond eyes, and the sun-browned skin that came with a life lived outdoors. The father sported an impressive floppy black mustache that twitched when he looked at the strange woman at his table. His eyes were green-brown, the dappled hazel color of the forest, warm and welcoming. He did not seem surprised to see her. "Howdy, young lady," he said, "glad to see you." He had seated himself at the other end of the table before Holly's attention turned to the son, who was still standing beside the back door with his hands clasped behind his back. His close-cropped black hair tended to curl on the top. But what gave Holly a start was her recognition of eyes so dark that she couldn't tell where the iris ended and the pupil began.

"It's you," she said.

He smiled. "I figured you'd be more comfortable accepting help from my ma than from some raggedy bum on a horse." He stepped forward and offered her a hand. She took it. "Call me Gee Dub."

Now that she had shed her coat and hat and scarves, Gee Dub was finally able to get a good look at the wary stranger he had found in the field. The voluminous outerwear had made the woman seem bigger than she was. She wasn't very substantial at all—small, thin, and hollow-cheeked. Her hair was the color of buckwheat honey, dark and thick and rich, with just a touch of amber to complement the color of her eyes. She had scraped it into a severe bun at the back of her head, practical for traveling.

Holly flinched when Alafair put a hand on her shoulder. She hadn't been aware that anyone was standing behind her. "It's a good thing he come got me, sugar, or you'd have froze clean to death out there in that field and nobody would have found your bones until spring. Now, don't you worry about anything but getting some good hot food into yourself. I declare, you need some meat on you if you mean to go traveling by foot in this weather. When you've eaten your fill, I'll get you into town. Or if you'd rather, you can have a sit by the stove for a spell, until you get warmed up."

Chapter Five

The food was hot and delicious and plentiful, but starving as she was, Holly was almost too tired to lift her fork. The family that she found herself dropped among was a lively crew, laughing and chatty. They seemed to understand that their guest needed to regain her strength before telling her story, so they happily took turns telling her about themselves. The only one who had nothing to say, Holly observed, was Gee Dub. He watched her quietly out of enigmatic dark eyes while his father talked.

"We've been out here for dog's years," Shaw was saying, "raising horses. I lost most of my work crew to Uncle Sam when the war came, but they're trickling back now, one by one." He cast a glance at Gee Dub, who did not glance back. "Our other boy, Charlie, is still in service, but now he's back in the States from Europe. He wrote us that when he does get out of the Army, he's going to travel around for a spell, see some of this country before he comes home. Gee Dub here has just been home for a few days. Still getting used to civilian life, aren't you, son?"

"That about sums it up," Gee Dub said.

Alafair leaned forward and placed her elbows on the table. "Now, you haven't said ten words together, Miz Johnson, but I can tell by the way you said them that you didn't grow up around here. Where you from?"

"New England. Maine. Portland, Maine."

Alafair and Shaw exchanged a glance before she said, "You're a long way from home. What brings you out to the wilds of

Oklahoma? I expect it wasn't a hankering to walk across the fields in the rain."

Holly developed a sudden interest in a crockery pot sitting on the windowsill. "I'm looking for my husband. He disappeared after the war ended. When I enquired of his sergeant, he told me that Dan's family lives in some place called Okmulgee. A few months ago I wrote to his mother, care of general delivery in Okmulgee, but I never heard back. So I thought I'd better come out here and find them. See if they know what happened to him." Her eyes narrowed as she scrutinized the pot even more closely. "I've been traveling from Maine for weeks."

"Surely you haven't been walking that whole long way."

Holly tore her eyes away from the pot and looked at Alafair. "No, ma'am, I mostly took the train, but I've had to stop for a while in one town or another and find work, until I had enough money to buy a train ticket to somewhere else."

"Well, you'll be glad to know that you're almost there, sugar. Okmulgee is but eighteen miles west of here."

Blanche was touched by the romance of Holly's quest. "Mama, surely we can give Miz Johnson a ride to Okmulgee."

The idea alarmed Holly. "Oh, no. Thank you, but no." She made a move to stand up. "I shouldn't have imposed on you…"

Alafair put out a hand. "Now, never mind, Miz Johnson. We're glad to help if you want, but how you finish your journey is up to you." She shot Blanche a warning look.

• • ● • •

The parlor was large and high-ceilinged, full of furniture that didn't match, with a potbellied stove in one corner and an upright piano in another. This time of year the furniture was grouped around the stove. Each chair had a small rag rug on the floor before it and a little table to its side, each covered with crocheted doilies and sporting a hurricane lamp or a candle. A large sewing basket sat beside one comfortable stuffed armchair. Holly pegged that one for Alafair's. A tall, locked, gun cabinet sat discreetly behind an open door that led to one of the bedrooms. A partially rolled quilting frame was suspended just under the ceiling, with a half-finished quilt stretched out on it. Holly didn't recognize the pattern.

The room was warm and homey, but as hard as she tried to stay engaged with the family's conversation, Holly felt herself nodding off. Her head fell forward and she jerked awake. It felt like she had only been out for a minute, but the parlor was deserted except for the dog snoring on a rug in front of the settee. Someone had placed a throw pillow behind her head and a blanket over her lap. She blinked at the window. It was dark and raining hard.

She could hear voices in the kitchen and stood up. Alafair, Shaw, and Gee Dub looked up at her when she appeared in the door.

"How long have I been asleep?"

"A couple of hours, sugar," Alafair said. "The girls have gone to bed, but you were just so worn out I didn't want to disturb you."

Holly pushed a stray lock of hair back over her ear. "My goodness, I must be leaving. I'm sorry to be such a bother."

Alafair stood up and gestured for Holly to take a chair at the table. "I declare, honey, you must be worn plumb to a nub after the day you've had. I've fixed up one of the beds in the girls' room just for you. Why don't you head on in? I'll bring you a pitcher of hot water so you can clean up a bit before bed."

The offer was only sensible, considering the time of day and the horrible weather, but this was not what Holly had planned at all. The idea of spending the night in the home of strangers she had come across on the road disturbed her.

Alafair read her expression. A glance, some wordless familial communication, passed between the three Tuckers, and Shaw pushed back from the table. "Come on in to the parlor, son," he said to Gee Dub. "Let the ladies talk."

Gee Dub's dark gaze lingered on Holly's face for a moment before he unfolded himself from his chair and followed his father into the parlor.

Once the men had left, Alafair resumed the conversation in a businesslike tone. "Miz Johnson, it's only a few miles to Okmulgee from here. I'll take you into Boynton first thing in the morning. You can get on the train there and be in Okmulgee in less than an hour."

"Mrs. Tucker, I can't afford a train ticket. I need to save what little money I have so that I can eat and perhaps pay for a place to stay for a few days until I find my husband. I've walked here all the way from Muskogee. I can walk from here to Okmulgee. Believe me, as far as I've come already, an eighteen-mile hike is nothing."

She expected Alafair to offer her the funds for a ticket and was prepared to refuse. But Alafair said, "Do you have folks in Maine who would wire you the money?"

"Not anymore."

Alafair sensed that there was a lot more to this tale than Holly was willing to tell her. That was her lookout, though, and none of Alafair's business. Even so…

"What if you can't find your husband before you run out of funds, Miz Johnson?"

"I'll find work in Okmulgee, then. Until I either find him or save enough for train fare back to Maine."

"Well, I won't hear of you walking all that long road to Okmulgee, a lone woman all by herself. Especially not in this weather. You've been lucky up to now that somebody hasn't knocked you on the head and stole everything you own. I'd feel a whole lot better if you'd let my husband or me carry you over there in the buggy. Do you know your mother-in-law's name?"

"Dan told me his father's name was Fern Johnson. I remember because I thought that was odd. I don't know the mother's name."

"Once you get there you can ask the operator at the Okmulgee telephone exchange if she knows of a Fern Johnson family in the area. If that don't work out, my husband's brother's family lives in Okmulgee. Charles owns a sawmill and one of his sons-in-law owns a haberdashery. You have working experience and it's plain that you have a lot of grit and perseverance. I'm sure that between the two of them they can scare you up a job of work, at least until you decide what you're going to do."

Holly's expression conveyed a cross between stunned disbelief at such generosity and skepticism about this chance-met stranger's motives. "I don't know what to say. I don't know how I can repay you."

Alafair leaned back in her chair. "Honey, if it was one of my daughters who was in such a fix, I hope someone would be kind enough to help her. Besides, I admire your grit. You let us help you out, now. Someday God will put a lost child in your path and you can help her."

• • ● • •

After Alafair settled her exhausted guest into an extra cot in the girls' bedroom, she returned to the parlor to find Shaw and Gee Dub with their chairs pulled up around the potbellied stove in the corner. Shaw was working on a ledger in his lap. Gee Dub was noodling around on his guitar, a quiet little ditty that Alafair didn't recognize. Neither man looked at her when she sat down in her armchair, but she was not fooled by their studied indifference.

"Did y'all hear?" she said.

"Part of it," Shaw admitted. "I heard her say she has no money."

"Dad," Gee Dub said, "who is the conductor on the Muskogee-Okmulgee milk run now? Is it still Joe Cecil?"

Shaw nodded. "Well, yes it is. As soon as Joe got back from San Antonio after the war, the gal who was filling in stepped aside and he got his old job back. Are you thinking your cousin Joe might let Miz Johnson hitch a ride to Okmulgee in the caboose?"

"He might. He let me do it once a few years back when I was heading to Okmulgee to do some temporary work for Uncle Charles in the sawmill. Maybe if I hang around the platform when the train comes through at eleven tomorrow I can catch him and bend his ear about it." He hesitated, then plowed on. "Even if I can't wrangle a free ride for her, a ticket from Boynton to Okmulgee is only a couple of dollars. I don't see why I couldn't advance her a loan."

Alafair opened her mouth to speak, but Shaw beat her to it. "I don't expect she'd take your money, son," he said. "She don't seem keen to get herself into debt."

"Well, maybe she'd be more likely to accept the money from Mama."

"I doubt it. Let the woman figure out her own plans, son."

Gee Dub didn't pursue it. Alafair picked up her mending from the side table and cast him a surreptitious glance. He didn't usually sit up with the family for so long. Since he had come home, he had been making his excuses and heading out to the bunk room shortly after supper.

"What do you think of our wandering lamb, son?" she said.

He looked up at her, but didn't stop playing. "Feel sorry for her. She's had some tough luck."

Shaw offered his opinion. "I don't think much of a man who'd desert his wife, if that's what he done."

"I'll drive her into Okmulgee tomorrow, if she'll let me. I'm not much good for anything else right now." Gee Dub's tone was casual.

Alafair shook her head. "She acts like she's spooked about something. I'm guessing she wouldn't feel comfortable taking a long ride with a man she don't know. You may have found her, but now it's best you leave her to me, son."

Gee Dub smiled and ended his tune with a flourish. He stood up. "Well, then, if that's how it is, Ma. I'm going to bed. I'll see y'all in the morning."

After Gee Dub left, the only sound in the house was the scratch of Shaw's pencil. Until Alafair said, "I think our boy has an eye for that young lady."

"She's married," Shaw said.

"He knows that."

"Well, then." *That's all there is to it.* Shaw did not need to point out that their son knew better than to set his sights on another man's wife. But Alafair wasn't entirely sure that the Gee Dub Tucker who had just left the house was the same Gee Dub Tucker who had gone to war.

Chapter Six

Rain was coming down steadily now, and Gee Dub was dripping wet by the time he made it back to the toolshed-cum-bedroom. Private Moretti had made it back before him and was stretched out on the extra bunk. Gee Dub shook out his hat and coat and hung them to dry on the peg beside the door.

"I figured you'd be asleep by now," Gee Dub said.

Moretti had something else on his mind. "Why are you keeping those cartridge boxes, Mr. Tucker?"

Gee Dub sighed and sat down on his own cot. He took his tobacco pouch out of his breast pocket and rolled himself a cigarette before he replied. "You been snooping around, I see."

"Not hard to see those yellow boxes sticking out from under your pillow."

Gee Dub managed a humorless laugh. "You of all people ask me that?"

"Well, maybe that's why I wanted to come, sir. Because of what happened in France."

Gee Dub lay down and exhaled a plume of smoke toward the ceiling. "I kind of figured that's why you showed up. You made a long trip for nothing, though."

"Well, maybe. But I'm here now. So you want we should go up to the house so you can introduce me to your ma and pa?"

Gee Dub turned his head to look at Moretti. God, he was young. Moretti reminded Gee Dub of his brother Charlie, though they didn't look alike at all. Charlie was tall and broad and fair of hair and blue of eye. Moretti was a skinny, pale, dark-haired teenager who said "wooder" instead of "water" and "yinz" instead of "y'all." But both ran headlong into action and were energetic and thoughtless as pups. He blinked at the young soldier a couple of times before his gaze slid back toward the ceiling. "I've been thinking about that. I haven't even told them you're here. I wonder why?"

"Are you ashamed of me, Lieutenant?" Moretti seemed to think that was a funny notion.

"You? No. It's just that right now I don't want to explain where I know you from. They'll ask questions. They'll want to know about France, and I'm not ready to tell them about it yet."

"Well, maybe you're right. Seems you ought to keep what happened over there separate from this life here."

"Give me a couple days."

"Don't worry about it, Lieutenant. I'll make myself scarce till you're ready."

"I hope Ma doesn't find out about you being here before I get the chance to tell her. She's liable to be taken aback."

"You are the master of understatement, Lieutenant. I would like to meet her, though. I never had a ma to dote on me like yours does."

"You were raised by your grandmother, if I remember right."

"My grandmother and my pa raised me and my brothers after my mother died. I was just six when she passed. I don't remember her too well."

"Grandmas are nice, though."

"Not mine. I don't think she was too happy about the situation, if I tell the truth. I expect she thought she was through with child-raising. She was pretty strict with us. Made us toe the line, that's for sure. But she stepped up when we needed her, I guess."

Gee Dub crossed his arms under his head. "Sometimes I try to imagine what it was like to grow up the way you did," he said to the ceiling. "Until they shipped our unit out to Baltimore, I had never seen a city bigger than Oklahoma City. I grew up playing in these fields here, and in the woods. The air is clean. I'd hate to think about my children having to play in those dirty streets of Baltimore. Of course, I expect there are some nice places in Baltimore. I never saw them, though."

Moretti shrugged. "Pittsburgh looks pretty much the same. But kids don't know no better. It was normal to me. My brothers and me had our fun."

"I reckon. Still, you don't know what you missed."

"Never will, I guess." He crossed his legs and grinned. "That's a pretty girl you found."

Gee Dub wasn't any happier with the new topic of conversation than he had been with the old. "You don't know nothing about it."

Moretti's response was mild. "Is that so?"

"Yes, Private, that is so. Howsoever pretty she is, she has other things on her mind. Like wondering if she's still married or not."

"But you wouldn't mind if she's not."

Gee Dub smiled. He wished he weren't so transparent. "Well, she is a pretty girl. She's a brave girl, too. I know better than to have designs on her, but that doesn't mean I can't appreciate what I'm seeing."

"You think she's scared of you?"

"Maybe. She's sure careful. I'm guessing that she's had some trouble along the way."

"Or maybe she don't want to like you too much, either."

Gee Dub shook his head firmly. "Don't even think it. No, she's had some trouble. Over in France I saw enough mistreated women to know what it looks like."

"And you think you can protect her?"

Gee Dub heaved a sigh. "I wish I could help her see that not all men think she's prey."

Moretti laughed at that. "Thing is, Lieutenant, there's a hell of a lot of men who do think of her just that way."

The girl in France was a teenager. She had probably been pretty once, but months of starvation and hardship had left her skeletal and hollow-eyed, with stringy black hair, bad skin, and few teeth. She still wanted to live, though. Gee Dub could tell that she did, because she was fighting the soldiers who had captured her. Not like that other woman he had come across weeks earlier, on the road to Cantigny. That woman had lain on her back in the mud, her skirt still scrunched up around her thighs, bloody. There was no helping that one. He had only been able to arrange her in a more dignified position before she died. But the girl in St. Lo still had some life left in her. And an unknown power—not that he much believed in Providence anymore—had put her in his path.

Gee Dub shook himself back into the present. Moretti's expression was knowing. "It's over, Lieutenant."

Gee Dub tried to rub the gooseflesh off his arms. "It'll never be over, Moretti."

• • ● • •

The sun was well up before Holly managed to drag herself out of bed the next morning. The old yellow dog had spent the night on the floor beside her bed and kept her company as she dressed. She had not slept so well in weeks. Not that she had wanted to give in so completely to exhaustion, but she had not been able to help herself. She expected it was because she felt safe for the first time in a while.

She made her way into the kitchen where she found Alafair at the stove, stirring a big pot of something that smelled delicious. Alafair threw her a glance over her shoulder.

"Good morning, honey. Did you sleep well?"

"I did, thank you. I didn't realize how tired I was. Where is everyone?"

"The girls are at school and my husband has gone out to the fields. Gee Dub is off on his own business. Sit down there and I'll fry you up a slice of mush and some bacon. You want some coffee? There's a pitcher of milk on the table."

Holly sat down and allowed Alafair to wait on her, still nursing the feeling that this whole situation was unreal. "I think I woke up about dawn and saw two children standing beside the bed, looking down at me. I think one of them was Grace, because she grinned at me and didn't have any top teeth. But the other one was a boy I didn't recognize. Maybe it was a dream, though. I drifted right back off."

Alafair made a noise that was half amusement and half exasperation. "You didn't dream it. The boy was my nephew, Chase Kemp. He's living for a spell with my daughter Mary and her baby Judy on the next farm over, while Mary's husband Kurt is still in the service and Chase's folks in Arizona get their law business off the ground. When the weather is too cold or rainy to walk, he comes over here, and me or Shaw take all the children into town for school in the wagon. Grace decided to show her cousin our exciting guest from all the way out in Maine, and they snuck off for a good look before I caught them."

Alafair didn't seem to be bothered by the incident, so Holly decided she wouldn't be, either. Alafair sat down at the table with a mug of coffee and watched Holly eat for a few minutes.

"What did you call this, Mrs. Tucker?" Holly poked at the golden slab of mush on her plate.

Alafair blinked. "That's cornmeal mush, honey. Haven't you ever eaten any before? Here, slap some butter on it, and try some of this sorghum." She stood up and began to fix the plate as though Holly were a five-year-old who couldn't manage to serve herself.

Holly took a bite and rolled it around on her tongue experimentally. "It reminds me of Indian pudding. My mother used to make it a lot, and sometimes I'd make for my father. But that is mixed with eggs and molasses and baked for a long time. Not fried, like this. I like to eat it in a bowl with milk."

"I make a kind of cornmeal pudding too, sometimes, but this is fast and easy in the morning." Alafair told her. "And we've been known to eat mush soft with milk and honey. But my youngsters like it best when it's fried. It's good with gravy, too."

"It's good," Holly admitted.

Alafair waited until Holly was on her second slab of mush before she said, "What are your plans, now, honey?"

"I wish that I had gotten up in time to hitch a ride into Boynton with Mr. Tucker when he took the children to school." She glanced out the kitchen window. The sky was still clouded, but the rain had stopped. "As soon as I've helped you clean up, I'll walk on into Boynton."

"There's no need to walk. It's like to start raining again any minute. I'll be happy to give you a ride to Boynton. Now, don't argue. It's no trouble at all. I need to buy some sugar, anyway. I'm baking today. You know, if you can see your way clear to wait until tomorrow, I'll give you a ride all the way into Okmulgee."

Holly shook her head firmly. "You have been so kind, but I'm so close now that I don't want to wait another day. I'll find my way to Okmulgee today."

Alafair's gaze wandered off for a moment. Holly knew she was scheming, trying to think of a way to persuade her to accept more help. She tried not to smile.

Alafair looked at her again. "You know, Gee Dub had an idea last night. Shaw's nephew Joe Cecil works as a railman on the milk run between Muskogee and Okmulgee. The train stops in Boynton at eleven. Once in a while, Joe lets one of my young'uns hitch a ride to Okmulgee in the caboose with him. Why don't we give that a try? I'm sure Joe would be happy to help, and it'd save your shoe leather, for sure."

The amber eyes widened. "I shouldn't let you do one more thing for me, Mrs. Tucker, but that is a tempting offer."

"I can imagine that you're mighty anxious for this long trip to be done."

"Oh, yes." Holly pushed her chair back from the table enough to enable her to reach into the pocket of her voluminous skirt and draw out a small leather folding wallet. She removed a paper sleeve that held a three-by-five snapshot and handed it to Alafair. "This is Dan."

Alafair studied the close-up of a man in uniform, his hair freshly shorn, no more than dark stubble. The eyes were light, maybe blue, but the black-and-white photograph made them look dove gray. He was not smiling, but he did look amused about something. "Nice-looking fellow," she said.

"A friend of his took this picture with his brownie camera a few days after we were married." Holly carefully replaced the photograph in her wallet and slid it back into her pocket before she replied. "I don't know what happened. Why he didn't come for me after the war. Maybe he meant to come here to Oklahoma and find a house for us, then send for me. Something must have happened to him before he could contact me."

"How long has it been since you've seen him?"

Holly decided to study her hands. "Almost a year. He was stationed near where I live. I had a war job at the shipyards in Portland and he was with Army procurement. That's where we met, in Portland. He was handsome and charming. I had never met anyone like him before. We were married within six weeks. It was just before he was shipped off to England. He wrote me the most wonderful letters for several months. Then the letters stopped. He had told me that his enlistment was up when the war ended. I figured that he was being mustered out and shipped home, and that he'd show up on my doorstep in a few days. Or weeks. But he didn't.

"He quit answering my letters, but they didn't come back, so he must have gotten them. If he was dead or missing the Army would have notified me, surely. Finally, I got the name of his sergeant from one of Dan's letters and wrote to him. He wrote back that he suspected Dan had gone back to Oklahoma because that's where his family is. I thought Dan was from Kansas. Olathe, Kansas. That's what he had told me, that he was a streetcar conductor in Olathe. But the sergeant's letter said that they didn't know where he was, either, and if I heard from him to let the sergeant know. As I told you, I've tried to wire Dan's parents, but I've never received a reply. Maybe I got something wrong with their name. If I can find out where they live, perhaps they can tell me what has happened."

Alafair listened to Holly's story with a growing feeling of dismay. Holly Johnson did not seem like a stupid girl, but rather than go through official Army channels to find out what had happened to her husband, she had taken the first clue she was given and started out on a two-thousand-mile trek to find someone who more than likely didn't want to be found. *What lengths people will go to in the name of love.*

"Miz Johnson," Alafair said. "Holly…"

Holly didn't let her finish. "You think he's abandoned me." It was not a question.

Alafair cocked her head to the side. "Do you really want to find him, sugar?"

"I don't know anymore." She was relieved to say it aloud at last. "I did when I first left Portland. I really did. But it's been such a long trip with no word. No joy. Where is he? If it weren't for this photograph I don't know if I would remember what he looks like. Am I still married or not? I have to know one way or the other."

Alafair stood up. "Don't worry about dishes. You go on and get your things and we'll leave for town as soon as you're ready. I'm going to take you by the jailhouse before the train comes. My husband's cousin is the town sheriff in Boynton. Tell him your story. He may be able to give you some advice about your rights."

Chapter Seven

Holly was prepared to be frightened of Sheriff Scott Tucker. As far as she was concerned, Oklahoma was a foreign country and she didn't know anything about how things worked here. She had a preconceived notion of what a small-town Southern lawman was like, and she had steeled herself to deal with someone who was threatening at worst, and at best, not inclined to take her seriously. She had encountered a lot of condescension on this journey. And not just from Southern lawmen.

But Scott Tucker didn't look like someone to fear. He was a man well into his fifties with a kind face and mild blue eyes who regarded her with curiosity when she walked into the jailhouse with Mrs. Tucker at her back. He laid aside the paper on which he was writing and clasped his hands together on the desktop. He nodded at Alafair, but his attention was on Holly.

"Hello, Miss," he said. "What can I do for you?" He unfolded one hand and gestured at the chair in front of his desk.

She accepted the invitation and sat down stiffly. "Sheriff, my name is Holly Johnson. I've come to Oklahoma from Maine, trying to track down my husband who disappeared after he was discharged at the end of the war. I have found out that his parents live in Okmulgee and I'm on my way there this morning. But Mrs. Tucker thinks it would be a good idea to ask your advice about my situation before I continue my search for Dan."

Sheriff Tucker straightened in his chair. "His name was Dan Johnson?"

She blinked, surprised at his response. "Yes, sir. Daniel Johnson. Have you heard of him? If he was going to Okmulgee, it is possible that he passed through Boynton on his way there."

Scott glanced at Alafair again, and Holly felt, more than saw, that Alafair had moved closer to her. Scott stood up. "Miz Johnson, I'm sorry to tell you that Private Daniel Johnson is the name of the man who was found dead beside the road just east of town a while back. That was a couple of months ago. Back in December, if I remember right." He walked over to a tall wooden file cabinet behind the desk and opened the top drawer.

Holly watched blankly as he rummaged through the drawer. She didn't know how to feel. Not particularly surprised. Not grief-stricken, or even very sad. If she felt anything at all, it was vague relief that this long quest could be nearly over.

"We figured that he died of the influenza," Scott was saying as he searched. "So many did throughout last winter. We buried him with all respect in the town graveyard. He was still in his uniform when he passed." When Scott turned to face her, he was holding a U.S. Army identity card in his hand. "This was found on him. He didn't have a poke or a wallet that we found. Just this and a beat-up identity tag in his pocket. I'm real sorry for your loss." He handed the card to her and left her with her thoughts. He gestured to Alafair, and she followed him to the other side of the room, where he made a show of pouring her a cup of coffee.

"I contacted the Army after we found the body," he said, keeping his voice low so Holly couldn't hear. "This Dan Johnson was a deserter. Seems he was wanted for killing another soldier in a fight. I did get hold of his parents in Okmulgee. After they found out what he did, they told me they'd just as soon forget him. That's why he's buried over in the graveyard yonder and not in Okmulgee."

"I declare! Their own son?" She was too shocked to keep her voice down, but Holly didn't turn around.

Scott shrugged. "Seems he was born sorry, to hear his dad tell it."

"Well, it's a sad thing. I hate the thought that he died all alone out in the cold, no matter what he did. Still, it sounds like yon child is well shet of him. And to tell you the truth, I think she may be relieved."

They made their way back to Holly's side. She had not moved since Scott handed her the identification card. She was still staring down at it, clutched in her hand.

"Miz Johnson?" Scott said. "Is there anything we can do for you now?"

Holly looked up. Her face was bloodless and the amber eyes were round as dollars. "Sheriff, this is not my husband. That's the right name, but I don't know who the man in this photo is."

• • ● • •

When Alafair turned her buggy into the gate of the big gray house on the edge of town, her mother-in-law was already standing on the porch, leaning against a pillar with a dishtowel in one hand and a wooden spoon in the other, waiting for her. Alafair wasn't surprised to see her. Half-Cherokee, half-Scots Sally McBride could sense things that others couldn't, especially when it came to her family. By the time Sally had led her through the parlor and into the kitchen, Alafair had told her all she knew about the mysterious Holly Johnson and the search for her missing husband. Sally deposited her at the kitchen table and set her up with dried-apple pie and milky tea before offering an opinion.

"It seems to me that if the child's husband is a killer and a deserter, she'd best leave well enough alone."

"Yes, but she's determined to find out if she's still wed."

Sally shrugged. "I don't know why. He run off and left her. She ought to find herself another man and get on with it."

"She's not a Cherokee woman, Ma. She can't just put her husband's saddle outside the door and call herself divorced."

"I don't know why not. Who's going to know, especially if the scoundrel is here in Oklahoma and she's all the way back in Maine?"

Alafair snorted. "Well, she doesn't see it that way." She took a bite of pie and chewed thoughtfully for a moment. "Scott says the first thing to do is to contact Johnson's folks in Okmulgee and see if they've heard anything from their son since Scott last talked to them. Then he has to find out who they've got buried out in the graveyard if it isn't Daniel Johnson."

"So your poor girl is right back where she started. What is she aiming to do now?"

"One step at a time, I guess. Scott is going to drive to Okmulgee this afternoon to talk to the Johnsons and maybe the police, and Holly is going to ride along with him. I told her that if things don't work out she's welcome to come back and stay with us a spell, at least until she knows what her next move is."

"You think she will?"

"I don't think she wants to, particularly. But I don't know what choice she has right now. She's flat broke. I offered to wire Charles about hiring her on at the sawmill. I think she'd be open to that. Tell you the truth, I can't decide whether I want her to come back here or not. I think Gee Dub has an eye for her. She's a pretty girl and I think he feels an obligation to look out for her, since he's the one found her on the road. In the normal course of things I'd be glad to see him interested in a nice girl. But Holly's got a peck of troubles and he don't need that right now."

Sally placed her elbows on the table and leaned toward Alafair. "How is Gee Dub? I haven't seen him since the day he got home and we all had dinner here at the house. I thought he looked like he didn't know whether to laugh or cry or split logs."

"Shaw says he just needs time to get readjusted. But something bad happened to that boy overseas. He's changed, Ma. Nobody sees it but me. But I don't know what to do for him." She put her fork down, troubled. "I went to clean his room the other day and found two boxes for rifle cartridges under his pillow, both empty but for one cartridge in one of the boxes."

"Forty dead men."

Alafair started and turned to see Shaw's stepfather, puckish, white-haired, little Irishman Peter McBride, standing in the kitchen door. "What did you say, Papa?"

Peter came into the kitchen and sat down at the table "Sally, *mo chroí*, I'd admire to have a slice of that pie." He turned to Alafair. "You've heard the tale about when I first got off the boat in America, darlin', and how I was met at the end of the gangplank by a tall man in a blue uniform who offered me a job and three squares a day if I'd join the cavalry and go off to tame the Arizona Territory. I was eighteen and had a thirst for adventure and no brains, so I said 'where do I sign?' They put me in a wagon with a dozen other stout lads and took us to training camp, where they gave me my own blue uniform and a rifle. Back in them days rifle cartridges came in a box of forty. So when my sergeant handed me my box he said, 'Here's your forty dead men, McBride. Don't waste them, 'cause the man you miss may be the one who kills you.'"

Chapter Eight

Holly had nothing to say on the long drive to Okmulgee with Scott Tucker in his Paige automobile. The constable made one or two gentle attempts to engage her, but when she only offered monosyllables in return, he mercifully left her alone. Though Scott had to do some fancy driving to avoid getting stuck on muddy stretches of road, the late February day had cleared off and was sunny and new-washed bright after the rain. But rather than admire the scenery, Holly spent most of the trip wondering how she had gotten herself into this situation. She was two thousand miles from home with no money, no husband, no prospects. There was always the possibility that her newfound in-laws would offer to take her in or at least assist her in some way. In truth she had no confidence that Dan's parents were going to be of any help. She could hardly believe they existed. *Sweet Lord, what an awful mess.*

The Lord hadn't been much help to now, either. Though she had to admit that He had placed the Tuckers in her path. They were not the first people to treat her kindly since she left Maine, but they were the first in a long time, and it disarmed her and made her nervous. She had fallen into the habit of being wary.

Well, in truth, it wasn't Sheriff Tucker who made her nervous. Or Mrs. Tucker or Mr. Tucker or all those cheerful little children. Holly banished the image of Gee Dub Tucker that rose to mind unbidden and made an effort to pay attention to her surroundings. Farms had given way to smaller and smaller homesteads. She could see the beginnings of neighborhoods and the odd business as they neared town.

Okmulgee was a much bigger town than Boynton. As they drove into the business district Holly was reminded of Muskogee, the bustling city where only two days earlier she had run out of money and begun walking. Scott drove directly to the police station and pulled into a parking space on the main street.

Scott had telephoned ahead and Chief Bowman was expecting them. The desk sergeant directed them down the hall to the Chief's office, where after introductions he invited them to sit and got down to business.

"Yes, Miz Johnson, I recognize him. I have had occasion to make your husband's acquaintance in the past and I believe I can direct you to his parents' house. I hadn't heard that he passed. I'm sorry for your loss." He handed Dan's photo back over the top of his desk before he picked up a note pad and began scratching out a map.

Scott held out the dead soldier's ID card for the Chief's inspection. "Well, we have us a mystery here, Mr. Bowman. A young fellow who died on the road outside of Boynton a while back had this on him. If you'll notice, the photograph ain't of the same man that Miz Johnson here, and now you, have both identified as the real Daniel Johnson. Have you ever seen this boy before?"

Bowman studied the identification card with interest. "I can't say I ever have. Well, now, this is a poser. Are y'all proposing that the real Dan Johnson is still alive? Because, if that's the case, I have to say I've never heard word of him coming back to town."

"That's just it, Chief Bowman," Holly said. "No one seems to know where he is. I'm relieved that the man I married really is Dan Johnson, but what has happened to him? And why was some poor flu victim in possession of Dan's ID card with his own picture on it? I'm praying that Dan's parents can solve this." Her voice caught in her throat and she fought back a spate of tears. "This is torment, Chief Bowman."

Both men hastened to hand the perhaps-widow their handkerchiefs and make soothing noises. "Miz Johnson, we will do everything we can to help you figure this out," Bowman said. He stood up and bellowed, "MacIntosh!" and the desk sergeant appeared in his door. "Mac, escort the young lady here to the couch in the D.A.'s office and get her a glass of water." He turned back to Holly. "The District Attorney is in court right now, so you can rest for a spell and gather your wits while I give Mr. Tucker directions to your in-laws' house."

Holly straightened and impatiently wiped her eyes. "I'd just as soon get on with it."

"Now, go on, dear lady," Bowman urged. "I want to talk to Mr. Tucker for a minute. We'll get you on the road directly. Besides, you'll feel better with a sit-down."

Holly sagged but acquiesced without an argument. Once MacIntosh had closed the door behind them, Bowman said, "All right, Scott. What's the story here?"

Scott related the information about Dan Johnson's desertion. Bowman was not surprised.

"Scott, I never was on intimate terms with that family, but Dan Johnson was no stranger to us here in the police department. Once he got to about fourteen, fifteen, he was always involved in something shady, mostly having to do with trying to part folks from their hard-earned money. He was a charmer, all right. Slicker than a slop jar and crooked as a dog's hind leg, that's for sure. His daddy is a fine upstanding citizen, too. Dan caused his poor folks no end of grief. Last I heard he got drafted and went off to wherever Uncle Sam decided his talents were most needed. I imagine it was a great relief for his parents to see the back of him. I never heard what happened to him after that. I don't even know if the folks are still alive. But if he went AWOL and his ID ended up on a corpse, I don't imagine that's a coincidence. Listen, if you find out anything after you drive over there, let me know."

• • ● • •

Scott insisted that they stop for luncheon at a little cafe on Sixth Street before going to the address Chief Bowman had given them. Holly protested, but Scott was adamant, and she reluctantly admitted that a nice bowl of chicken and dumplings did make her feel better. Perhaps she would even be able to cope with whatever they were going to find after Scott pulled up to the tree-shaded frame house a few blocks from downtown.

Holly was standing behind Scott when he knocked on the door, but she didn't need to be told that the natty man with blue eyes who answered was Dan's father. He was the spitting image of his son. Holly felt her knees go weak and she grabbed the back of Scott's coat to keep from falling. Scott was in the middle of explaining their presence to Mr. Johnson but put a steadying arm around her shoulders without looking at her, as though it were the most normal thing in the world to do.

Fern Johnson opened the screen and stepped out onto the porch. "You're the one who wired us from Boynton last December."

Scott nodded. "I am." He held out Holly's photograph. "Do you recognize this man?"

"That's Dan. That's my son. But your wire said Dan was dead."

"Mr. Johnson, it's a complicated story and we need to talk to you about it."

Johnson looked at the pale woman Scott was holding up and his forehead wrinkled. "And this gal says she's Dan's wife?"

Something about his tone made Holly bristle. "I *am* Dan's wife."

Johnson gave them both an intense once-over. "Well, I guess y'all better come in, then."

He ushered them into a neat, doily-filled parlor, where a bent, desiccated woman was standing beside the door, wringing her hands. Holly blinked at her. Dan had never mentioned a grandmother. Whoever she was, she had obviously heard everything, for Scott and Holly had barely lowered themselves onto the green horsehair settee when she burst out, "Y'all are lying! What are you doing here?"

Johnson grabbed the woman's shoulders. "Hang on, now, Lucy. Sit down. Let the sheriff talk."

She shook him off. "This ain't right. My son is dead."

Not Dan's grandmother after all, but his mother. She may not have been as old as she first appeared but she was obviously very ill. She sank into an armchair, too weak to stand any longer. She pointed at the woman on her settee with such vehemence that if her finger had had been a gun, that would have been the end of Holly. "You! What are you playing at? Are you trying to get money? You aren't Dan's widow. Dan's widow lives across the street."

Holly shot Sheriff Tucker an amazed glance. He looked as taken aback as she felt. "What are you saying?" she managed. "Dan was married before?"

Mr. Johnson had a death grip on his wife's arm. "Him and Pearl were married before he went off to the Army and were married to the day he died," he said. "I don't know who you are, young lady, but you aren't my son's widow."

How she didn't faint, Holly never knew. A flood of panic flushed every rational thought out of her head. She leaped up, banged out the front door and took off down the street as fast as her legs would carry her.

Scott hurried after her, calling her name, but Holly was half-way down the block before Scott even got out the front door. He hesitated on the porch steps, watching in awe as her figure retreated into the distance. *For such a small person*, he thought, *she can really move fast.*

Well, where else would she go but back toward Boynton, and how far could she get? Scott still had plenty to discuss with Dan Johnson's gobsmacked parents. Once he'd finished questioning the Johnsons, he'd pick up Holly on the way out of town.

● ● ● ● ●

"Sheriff, I think you'd better explain. If the man you buried last December wasn't Dan, then who was he?"

"That's what we're trying to find out, Mr. Johnson."

Johnson lifted a hand to his forehead. "Well, then what you are saying is that Dan is alive."

"Maybe. Maybe not. All we know for sure is that the dead soldier we found by the side of the road had Dan Johnson's military identification papers on him, but the photograph had been changed. So either Dan Johnson took the soldier's ID, or the soldier took Dan's ID, or the two of them traded IDs before the soldier died. No matter which, this means that your son's whereabouts are unknown."

"Well, we sure don't know where he is." Johnson was firm about that. "Dan had a habit of consorting with unsavory types. I would not be surprised if he hooked up with a fellow deserter somewhere along the line who likely killed my son and stole his identity papers. Dan knew his mother is sick. If Dan was still living he would certainly have found some way to contact his mother, and that has not happened. That's the main reason I'm inclined to believe that Dan really is dead. He has not tried to get in touch with his mother."

Scott could not interpret the look that Johnson gave his wife when he said that. Sympathy, perhaps, for having given birth to such an unworthy child? The turn of events had definitely upset Mrs. Johnson no end. She was perched nervously on the edge of her chair, twisting her handkerchief in her lap when she wasn't using it to dab at the tears dribbling down her sunken cheeks.

"But this woman who claims to be Dan's widow," she said, her voice husky with emotion, "what can she be playing at? What does she think she's going to gain from pretending to be married to my boy?"

"She's not playing, ma'am," Scott assured her. "She is in possession of a marriage license issued by the state of Maine which states that she and one Daniel Bell Johnson were married official-like last year."

"She must have married the impostor who was pretending to be Dan."

"I'm afraid not. The photograph of Dan that I showed you belongs to her. He married her before he was posted overseas, then he never contacted her after he was shipped back to the States. She travelled on her own all the way out here from Maine to try and figure out what happened to him. She didn't know he was married, or that he was AWOL, or that he was wanted for manslaughter."

"Well, he was married, and to a wonderful, upstanding girl. That woman from Maine must be an awful temptress to persuade my boy to commit bigamy."

Mr. Johnson gave his wife's shoulder a shake, half sympathy, half exasperation. "Hush, now, Mother. Hush. You'll have to forgive my wife, Sheriff. She is not well. Besides, she never could believe anything bad about Dan, no matter what evidence presented itself."

Scott could tell by her expression that Mrs. Johnson was gearing up to defend her baby. He was not in the mood to hear it and spoke before she could get started. "Since Dan was already married, the young lady who just lammed it out of here is no longer of concern, I reckon. She wanted to find out if she was still married and she found out, all right. The question now is what has happened to Dan Johnson and who is the fellow we buried? I have a couple of ideas that I'll pursue when I get back to Boynton. I'm sorry to be raking this all up after you figured it was over and done. If by some chance you hear from Dan, or hear of him, you'd be well advised to notify the police. I spoke to Chief Bowman over to the police department before we came here, so he is already apprised of the situation."

Mrs. Johnson bit her lip, but Mr. Johnson gave a resigned nod. "Sheriff, Dan's real widow, Pearl, is engaged to be married this summer. It took a while, but she was able to move on with her life. What is this going to mean for her?"

"I don't know, Mr. Johnson, but if I was her, I'd consult a lawyer."

Chapter Nine

After Gee Dub learned that Holly had finally gone to Okmulgee with Scott, he set out to ride up his hill after dinner, as usual. Instead, he found himself riding up and down the road to Okmulgee for hours. He rode Penny a mile this way and two miles that way, until he had ridden nearly all the way to Morris, a mere five or six miles from Okmulgee. He was about to turn back toward home when he caught sight of a figure in the distance coming toward him. A woman. He reined in and simply sat there on Penny's back, watching the woman come closer and closer.

Could it be?

He would not believe his own eyes. He was never going to see Holly Johnson again and he was not seeing her now. Too often over the past few months he had found himself immersed in a world that turned out to be an illusion. He sat there for a long while, wistfully enjoying the sight of the phantasm coming toward him, unwilling to return to reality.

The illusion of the lion-eyed woman faded and he found himself back in the command bunker, sitting on his cot. It was dark, the only light coming from the single kerosene lantern on the makeshift desk that Lieutenant Anderson had created out of a big rock, some bricks, and a piece of scrap wood. Where was Anderson, anyway? It was pounding rain. Water was dripping through the waterlogged log-and-daub roof, creating a puddle in the middle of the floor. The air smelled of mud and mold, gunpowder and unwashed bodies. And tea. Sharma was squatting over the camp stove, brewing tea. Sharma was the strangest little man that Gee Dub had ever met, and Gee Dub had met plenty of odd people from odd countries since he had been overseas. Frenchmen, of course. Canadians, Brits, and Australians, who always sounded like they were leaning against something when they spoke. He liked working with the British enlisted men, though he could hardly understand what they were saying most of the time. They were tough and funny. He didn't care for the officers much, since it seemed that most of them didn't care for Americans. Anderson was all right. Distant, but that suited Gee Dub.

Sharma was Anderson's servant, as far as Gee Dub could tell. He took care of Anderson's kit with as much care as a wife would have done, and since Gee Dub had moved into the command bunker, Sharma took care of him as well. It was an odd sensation. Sharma said he was an Indian, and Gee Dub had laughed and told him that he was an Indian, too, though he didn't expect they belonged to the same tribe.

Funny little guy. Gee Dub was curious about him, but Anderson was rather proprietary about his servant, so Gee Dub didn't presume. By that time he had learned it was a mistake to cultivate relationships.

Sharma was the first non-Christian that Gee Dub had ever met. He liked the man, but he just naturally figured he was on his way to hell with all the other pagans. That was before he knew any better.

After the shell hit the trench and buried the six Geordies whom it didn't blow to kingdom come, Gee Dub, Anderson, and Sharma had spent most of the afternoon digging out bodies. They managed to disinter four men before they smothered. The other two weren't so lucky. That was one of the low points for Gee Dub, and Anderson didn't take it well, either. Late that night, Sharma told them about the "return." That's what Gee Dub called it. Sharma called it a wheel that we go round and round on, coming back and living life over and over until we get it right. Gee Dub had never heard such an outlandish notion. But he did like the idea. There was certainly no mercy or justice or any second chances on this side of death. It would be nice if there were some in another life.

Gee Dub woke with a jolt. He was still in the saddle. The woman had stopped walking and was gazing at him uncertainly. Holly had covered nearly a quarter-mile since the last time he was aware.

He blinked to clear his eyes and leaned over the saddle horn, his forehead wrinkling. She was not an illusion.

"Holly?"

"What are you doing here, Gee Dub?"

He slid down off the horse without realizing what he was doing. Holly's eyes were red and practically swollen shut.

The sight made Gee Dub forget himself. "Good Lord! What the hell happened to you?"

Her lips thinned and she looked away.

He seized her by the upper arms and she winced. He backed off, suddenly aware that he was looming over her. He raised his hands in a soothing gesture. "Where's your kit?"

She looked around, surprised that she wasn't carrying her carpetbag. "I guess I left it at Mrs. Johnson's house. I just wanted to get out of there. They can keep it. I'm never going back."

"Where's Scott? What happened to you, Holly?"

She drew herself up and looked him in the face, small and vulnerable and brave. "It seems I was never married, after all."

Gee Dub had pretty much gotten the picture as soon as he saw the state she was in.

"Daniel…" She laughed, but there was no humor behind it. "He already had a wife when he married me. What an idiot I am. So stupid, so stupid."

Gee Dub could hardly see her through the sudden haze of red before his eyes. He made a move to remount, but Holly seized his arm. "Don't you dare. It's none of your business."

He acquiesced, but it was hard for him to speak through the knot of fury in his throat. "Come on, then. You're going back home with me."

"I can't. I can't impose on your folks any more than I have."

"Well, I guess you are stupid, then. What else are you going to do, woman?"

"Don't you talk to me like that. I've had about all the disrespect I can take today. I'm going to walk back to Boynton and wire my aunt in Bangor. She always liked me. Maybe she'll find a way to send me some money. And if she doesn't, I'll find a job somewhere."

"Who's going to hire you looking like you've been dragged through a mud hole and stomped on? Let me give you a ride."

"Leave me alone." Her face was flushed and she was blinking rapidly to contain her tears.

Gee Dub backed up a step. "All right, then," he said, exasperation heavy in his voice.

Holly squared her shoulders and resumed her march down the road without a backward glance. Gee Dub mounted up and swung Penny's head around to follow the furious woman at a desultory walk.

They carried on like that for nearly a mile before Holly finally threw a glance over her shoulder.

"Leave me alone," she said.

"This is a public road. I can ride on it if I want."

"I don't need your help."

"I can tell you have everything under control."

She picked up her pace. "Gracious! You are infuriating!"

They marched on in silence for another half-mile before Holly sat down in the middle of road without warning and burst into tears. Gee Dub let her cry for a moment before he got down out of the saddle and offered her a linen square from his back pocket.

She looked at it as though she had no idea what it was.

"It's clean," he said.

She snatched it out of his hand and buried her face in it. "Blasted tears," she mumbled. "The saltwater stings my sore eyes."

"Are you going to come with me now?"

She glowered at him from under her hat brim. "Only if you clearly understand that I am going to pay your family back as soon as I get money."

"You don't owe us anything."

"Do you understand what I just said?"

Gee Dub fought a sudden inexplicable desire to laugh. "Yes, ma'am. Now get up out of the dirt." He held out a hand and helped her to her feet.

● ● ● ● ●

Alafair didn't bother offering her opinion to either Holly or Gee Dub as she bent over the basin of hot water on the kitchen floor and laved Holly's bloody feet. A five-mile run on a rough road had taken its toll. Holly's sturdy brogans, which had served her well for two thousand miles, were coming apart at the seams and had been left on the back porch.

Gee Dub leaned on the kitchen doorpost with his arms crossed, keeping his distance, while staying close enough to see what was happening. Alafair had learned five grown children ago that when it came to matters of the heart, young people were not going to listen to advice, reason, or plain sense. She just kept her head down and fussed over Holly's physical wounds. There was nothing she could do about the young woman's wounded heart.

"Now I know why I wasn't getting his money from the Army," Holly said, more or less to Alafair but loud enough for Gee Dub to hear. "He was having his pay sent to her. He told me that since I was working and didn't need it, he was having it deposited in a savings account so we could buy a house when he got out. She must have got the widow's benefit, too."

"If he deserted, she didn't get his insurance," Gee Dub said.

Holly's expression indicated that she thought that was small comfort.

Alafair gently lifted Holly's blistered feet out of the water and onto her aproned lap to dry them with a soft towel. "Gee Dub, hand me that salve, there." She gestured vaguely toward the counter. "Miz Johnson, do you aim to go have a talk with the other wife?"

Holly made a surprised sound. "Why? You think I can make her split Dan's back-pay with me?"

"Well, at least you deserve enough to get you home again, if that's what you want."

Gee Dub had taken advantage of his mother's summons and seated himself at the table, the better to join the conversation. "If I were her, I'd think it was worth it to give you train fare. I'd want to see the back of you as quick as possible."

Holly's bottom lip poked out, stubborn. "I don't want anything from them."

"You could still go back to Okmulgee and work for my Uncle Charles," Gee Dub said.

She sighed. "It's a generous thought and I certainly need the job. But I just can't go back there where people might recognize me for the fool I am."

"We have a slew of relatives and friends in Boynton," Alafair said. "Surely one of them would be able to scare up a job for you. My oldest daughter, Martha, and her husband own a land and title company."

Gee Dub lifted an eyebrow. "Might want to let Martha and Streeter decide about that, Ma." Alafair was as quick to offer her children's charity as she was her own. The children were generally good-natured about it, but Martha had already told Gee Dub that the McCoy Land and Title Company would have to give the men who went to the war their old jobs back before they could think about hiring anyone new.

Alafair was undaunted. "What work are you looking for, Miz Johnson? What sort of jobs have you had before?"

"Well, I had to take care of my father after my mother died. I can cook and clean and sew as well as anyone. During the war I did several jobs at the shipyard, whatever they needed. I started out as a file clerk in the procurement office. That's where I met Dan. But at night I took a typing course, so most of the time I was in procurement I was a typist. I can operate a switchboard, and for a little while, right at the end of the war, I worked as a welder."

"A welder?"

"Yes, ma'am. Once I learned how not to burn my hands off or blind myself, it wasn't such a hard job, and it paid a lot better

than typing and filing. They put six of us girls on the night shift
so that the experienced men could have the better hours. The
worst part was what we had to put up with from the men on
our shift. But that's always the way it is. I made a lot of money
and I tried to save it, but most of it went to the doctors and the
other bills when my father got sick and couldn't work anymore.
Then he died and most of the rest went to bury him. That's when
I decided to find Dan. I only had enough money left to buy a
train ticket to St. Louis."

Gee Dub had been listening to this recitation with a combination of admiration and growing amusement. The image of
little Holly welding iron plates onto a battleship delighted him
no end. "Sounds like you have job skills to spare. Maybe Mr.
Turner could use her in his new automobile repair shop, Ma."

Alafair brushed the remark away. "Quit teasing, son. Still,
there's something to what he says, Miz Johnson. With all your
experience, we ought to be able to find you a job of work around
here with no trouble."

"I can hardly think right now, Mrs. Tucker. If you'll grant
me one more kindness, I could surely use a rest. Oh, and you'd
better stop calling me Miz Johnson. Seems I'm not Holly Johnson, after all. From now on I'd better be Holly Thornberry, like
I was born."

"Thornberry! I like the way Thornberry goes with Holly,"
Alafair said.

Holly took the soft cotton socks that Alafair offered and
carefully slipped them onto her damaged feet. "Yes, that was my
mother's clever idea. It's better than Johnson, though."

Alafair stood up. "I reckon. Now, the bed you slept in last
night is still made up. You go on in and have a lie-down. I expect
Scott will be by to see if we've found you after you ran off from
him. He'll probably have some news."

Chapter Ten

The afternoon was well along by the time Scott came chugging down the drive in his Paige with Holly's carpetbag on the seat next to him. Once he was assured that Holly had indeed made her way back to the farm with Gee Dub's help, Scott sat down with her in the parlor to tell her what he had discovered in Okmulgee. Supper was on the stove and the men were due in from the fields any minute, but Alafair had no intention of leaving Holly on her own to hear what could be depressing news. She had seated herself in her armchair, next to Holly, with yet another grandchild in her lap, a bouncy two-year-old blonde named Judy Lucas. Holly didn't know this one. Alafair and Scott were discussing something Holly only heard with half an ear while she studied the toddler, bemused. Infant grandchildren seemed to pop up out of the ether around here. Blanche, Sophronia, Grace, and Alafair's nephew Chase Kemp had all dragged kitchen chairs into the parlor and lined themselves up next to the wall, the better to eavesdrop. Alafair made a move to send them off, but Holly said she didn't mind. So a silent and wide-eyed Greek chorus of children would serve as witnesses to the proceedings. Holly briefly wondered where Mr. Tucker was. Or Gee Dub.

"I'm sure glad to see that you didn't run clean back to Maine, Miz Johnson," Scott said. "When I didn't come across you on the road back to Boynton, I feared you'd gotten yourself so lost that nobody would ever see you again."

Holly's cheeks reddened. "All I could think was that I had to get away from there. That's all. I didn't have a plan."

"I understand. Miz Johnson…I mean Miz Thornberry, I didn't want to tell you at first, but back in the winter, when I thought that our dead soldier was your husband, I contacted his folks by wire and they told me they didn't want to claim his body because he was a coward and a murderer who deserted the Army. If they had seen the body and realized it wasn't their son, we wouldn't be in this situation. I didn't know Johnson was married. After you scarpered, I went to see the…other widow. I'm sorry to confirm that her and Dan were indeed married in church a month before he got drafted. She showed me the license. So I'm afraid your marriage wasn't legal and you don't have any claim to his property. Which, as near I could find out, there ain't any, anyway. I have to say that…" he hesitated, unwilling to say "the other widow" again. "Pearl Johnson is not living in heartbreak. She's found her another man and aims to remarry next fall. She was knocked for a loop when she heard that Dan might not be dead."

Holly straightened in shock. "Wait a minute. You think Dan really is still alive?" She felt foolish the moment she uttered the words. When she found out that someone else was buried in Dan's grave, she had not seriously considered the implications.

Scott swallowed his words and sat back. His expression was compassionate. "It's possible, ma'am. Once I knew that the man we buried isn't Daniel Johnson, I had a real close look at that identification card. Somebody probably scraped off the original photograph and glued Dan's on. Whoever it was did a good job. Now I'm guessing that we have a case of switched identities, here, so the next thing we have to do is discover who is buried in yonder graveyard."

"But how in the world are you going to do that, Sheriff? Even if you dug him up…" Holly glanced at the row of children by the wall and didn't finish the thought.

"We may be in luck, there," Scott said. "The man we buried had an Army ID disc in his pocket. I kept it, but the disc was partially defaced. Looked like it had been struck with a hammer. The name and rank were too damaged to read very easy so I didn't much try. I didn't think much of it at the time. But there is a serial number on it. I never did bother to cross-check the number with the Army since I had his card, and the picture on it was definitely the dead man."

"If Dan went to so much trouble to change ID cards, why deface the name on the disc instead of just trade that with his own, too?" Alafair pointed out.

"That's just it, Alafair. I don't think the ID tag was defaced on purpose. It was probably some kind of accident. Maybe it deflected a bullet. The soldier had taken it off and put it in his pocket. If it was Dan who made the ID switch, could be he didn't know the disc was there. As soon as I get back to town I'll fish that tag out and have a good look at it. Maybe I can make out a name with my magnifying glass. Even if I can't, the Army will be able to tell me who belongs to that serial number." He slapped his hands on his thighs. "All right. Now, as for you, young woman, looks like you've come to the end of your search. Whether Dan Johnson is alive or not is none of your lookout anymore. You're a free unmarried lady. Have you given any thought to your next move?"

The question made Holly laugh. "Sheriff, I have no idea. I've been talking to Mrs. Tucker about finding a job here until I can earn enough money to go back to New England. Other than that…"

"Well, you're in good hands. Let me know if there's anything I can do for you."

"Will you keep me informed about your investigation?"

Scott and Alafair exchanged a glance before Scott said, "Sure I will, if that's what you want."

She lifted one shoulder in a weary shrug. "He wasn't much, but I thought he was my husband for over a year. I would like to know what happened to him."

• • ● • •

The next morning, Holly helped Alafair and the girls get breakfast ready. No one asked her to pitch in, nor did she ask permission. She simply didn't know what else to do with herself. Alafair didn't remark on it. She just ordered her around in the same businesslike fashion as she did her own daughters. Holly found that oddly comforting.

Holly was grateful when Alafair handed her a basket and directed her to the henhouse to gather eggs. She pulled on her coat and stepped out into the backyard, accompanied by her constant companion, Charlie Dog. She paused for a moment to breathe in a lungful of crisp February air. She could see her breath in the air when she exhaled. The sun was not quite up, but the horizon was a shocking pink with a layer of cream on top, decorated with the dark frilly outlines of the bare trees in the copse a few yards behind the house. She looked for the henhouse in the general direction that Alafair had pointed before sending her outside, and was just starting toward a low building surrounded by chicken wire when she saw that Grace—she of the black braids and missing front teeth—had followed and was watching her from the porch steps.

Grace grinned her toothless grin when she realized that she had been spotted. "I'se wondering where you were going."

"I'm going to gather some eggs for breakfast. Would you like to come with me?"

Grace didn't have to be asked twice. She flounced off the porch and took Holly's free hand in hers, a move so natural that Holly hardly noticed.

"Is it usually your job to gather the eggs in the morning? Am I taking your job?" Holly said.

"No. Well, sometimes Mama sends me out, but usually that's Fronie's job. I just figured I'd fill up my ears with some quiet this morning before breakfast, is all, and then I seen you."

Grace trotted along beside Holly, swinging their clasped hands in wide arcs. "I'm glad you let me come. Daddy said you may be needing some extra peace and quiet for a spell after your disappointments."

That surprised Holly. "Did he, now?"

"Would you rather be alone? I promise I won't prattle on."

"Well, if you aren't going to prattle, I expect it'll be all right for you to come and help me out."

Grace gave her a sidelong glance, judging the level of humor in her voice and deeming it sufficient. "Sometimes I like to come out here and be alone myself. It's hard to be on your own when you've got so many brothers and sisters and cousins and nieces and nephews."

"I would imagine."

They reached the henhouse, and Grace imperiously ordered Charlie Dog to sit, before leading Holly through the chicken-wire gate. Holly had to bend down to make her way inside the coop. It was much bigger than the little chicken house that she had kept on the tiny patch of ground behind their house in Portland, but the smell of feathers and hay and the rustle and cluck of the hens were familiar. She and Grace took up their conversation along with their task.

"Do you have brothers and sisters?" Grace said.

"I don't. I'm an only child."

"That must be lonely."

"Sometimes it was," Holly admitted. "But I never knew any different."

"I like the way you talk. When you say 'Miz Tuck-ah', and 'good mawnin' and 'ayeh' instead of 'yes'."

"I like the way you talk, too. When you say 'y'all' and 'howdy' and 'Tuck-errr' like a dog growling."

That made Grace laugh. "I been learning to play the guitar."

Holly blinked at the shift of topic. "Have you?"

"Mama said I could practice on Gee Dub's guitar while he was gone."

"Well, he wasn't using it."

Grace put her three eggs in Holly's basket and sat down on an empty roost box. She crossed one leg over the other in a surprisingly adult manner and grasped her top knee with both hands. "I missed hearing him play," she said.

"Sounds like you came up with a good solution."

She shrugged. "His guitar is kindly too big for my hands, so I'm not too good with the chords yet. But I can pick out some songs all right. Mama taught me a couple tunes."

"What's your favorite?"

"Right now I like 'Pretty Polly.'"

"I don't know that one."

"That's kind of a sad song. I mean, old Willie stabs his love and all. It's got a nice tune, though. I like 'Cotton-Eyed Joe,' too." She began to sing in a piping voice that caused a stir among the hens. "If it wasn't for Cotton-Eyed Joe, I'd have been married a long time ago…"

"You like songs about unhappy lovers, don't you? Are you pining for some boy?" There was a laugh in Holly's voice.

"I like songs I can play," Grace said, matter-of-fact. "You want me to play you something after breakfast?"

"I don't know. Are you any good?"

"Not particularly."

"Well, I'd love to hear you anyway. Let's see if we still have time after breakfast. I plan on starting my journey home as soon as I can."

"Why, that'll be sad," Grace said, "We're just getting to know you."

Chapter Eleven

Holly spent the morning washing out her laundry on the back porch and airing out her carpetbag, after which she insisted on helping with housework while she waited for her clothes to dry before repacking for her journey.

Late in the morning, Alafair took Holly out to the garden to check on the progress of her crops. On the edges of the garden, a few little seedlings were poking up, but in a sunny plot on the south-facing side of the house, some of the lettuces, radishes, and scallions were almost big enough to pick.

Alafair nodded, satisfied, and handed Holly a willow basket before the two women knelt down in the dirt. "I ought to let these here greens do a little more growing, but if we just take some outside leaves, I think we can get enough for a salad, especially with some little radishes and a green onion or two."

"Where I come from, it'll be May, maybe June, before it's warm enough to start an outside garden." She pulled a nice-sized red radish out of the ground and held it up for Alafair's inspection. "Look at this," she said, delighted.

"See if you can find a few more like that. I declare, Shaw and the children will be mighty happy to see a green salad on the table. You know how it is after a long winter with no fresh food right out of the garden. Once the carrots come up, my family eats so many of them that I swear their noses turn orange." She examined the lettuce plants closely. "I don't think I can get a half-peck of lettuce without pulling up the plants. I saw some young chickweed back near the woods. I'll add some of that."

Holly sat back on her heels. "Every spring me and my mother would go hunting for fiddlehead ferns. How I always looked forward to that. She'd cook them up on the stove in a little butter."

"I never heard of fiddlehead ferns. I reckon they don't grow down here."

"Oh, that's too bad. That's how I knew winter was over, when it was time to forage! I lived right on the shore. All year my mother and I could go down to the cove and go clamming. My favorite is lobster, though. We'd get lobsters at the dock after the boats came in, maybe two, three times a week. Lobsters are cheap, poor-people food, but I love lobster meat."

"I never have eaten a lobster," Alafair said. "I've seen pictures, though. Them claws look like they could snap your hand right off. They look like great big crawdads. I wouldn't want to meet one in the dark! My boy Charlie loves crawdads. Made himself a crawdad rake. We've got crawdads galore in the cricks and ponds around here. I've never been to Maine, but it sounds like it's mighty different from here."

"It surely is." Holly's eyes misted and she looked away, distressed. "I miss my mother."

Alafair reached across the row of radishes to squeeze her hand. "It's all right, honey." She set her basket on the ground and sat down, crossing her legs Indian style. "You know, back a few years ago, Blanche come down with an awful lung infection and the doctor said the best way to fix her was to go to Arizona for a spell. So her and me and her daddy took the train all the long way out there and stayed with my sister in Tempe for a few weeks. I had the idea that Arizona isn't all that different from Oklahoma, but I couldn't have been more wrong. I felt like I had gone to the moon, it was so different. I didn't recognize one tree or bush that grew wild, and the food that folks ate! Now of course, my sister Elizabeth grew up eating the same way I did, so most of her cooking wasn't that strange. But her neighbors that grew up in Arizona cooked food like I had never eaten before. It was mighty tasty, and sometimes I still get a hankering for a tamale. But there just ain't no food that will satisfy you like the food you grew up with." She gave Holly's hand a little shake. "That's because your mama's food tastes like love. And it is, because when somebody who loves you makes something with her own hands, it gets transferred right into the food, and nothing else will ever compare."

• ● ● ● •

At dinnertime, Alafair showed Holly how to make red-eye gravy by pouring black coffee into the inch of drippings left after frying slabs of fatty ham. The food here in Oklahoma was as foreign to Holly as Chinese. Everything was fried, fatty, sugary, and rolled in cornmeal. She longed for a bowl of fish chowder or some nice steamed lobster or clams. The memory of clam-digging with her mother arose again, and she was overcome with homesickness. She missed the smell of the ocean and the fresh feel of the wind off the Atlantic, the cry of the seabirds and the creak of the hawsers that moored the fishing boats down at the harbor. She dragged her attention back to the skillet on the stove in front of her and ran the back of her hand over her eyes before a tear could drop into the hot grease. She followed Alafair's instructions and poured the coffee-fat-ham bits combination into a serving dish, where the coffee sank to the bottom and the grease floated to the top. No flour, no thickener of any sort. Holly felt her nostrils thin at the sight. They called it "gravy," but it seemed to her like an awful waste of good coffee.

Holly was just setting the table when Gee Dub and Mr. Tucker came into the kitchen from the barn. They were accompanied by a tall, red-haired young man whom she had not seen before.

Gee Dub made the introductions as the men were seating themselves at the table. "Miz Thornberry, this fellow is Trenton Calder, Scott's deputy. He's also aiming to marry my sister Ruth, so after next month he will be my brother-in-law, to boot."

Before he sat down, Trent held out a hand. "Miz Thornberry, happy to meet you at last."

"Mr. Calder. I do believe everyone in Boynton is related in some way to this family."

"That is our aim," Alafair said. "Trent, what brings you out here in time for dinner? Do you have some news for Miz Thornberry?"

"I do," Trent said, and Holly instantly lost her appetite.

• • ● • •

The serial number on the identification disc had been the key. Scott had wired the number to the military registration office in Oklahoma City and had had his answer in a matter of hours. "Our dead soldier," Trent said, "or at least the man who had previously owned the ID tag, was one Harvey Stump from Council Hill, Oklahoma. Harvey was discharged on December 10, 1918, in Baltimore, which is very near the last date and location we have for the deserter Daniel Johnson. Scott figures that Dan took up with poor old Harvey, who was none the wiser about Dan's status, and they traveled together down to Oklahoma. Now, we haven't figured out yet how Harvey ended up dead of the flu on the road between Muskogee and Boynton with Dan's identification card on him."

Gee Dub said, "It sounds like Harvey died of the grippe and Dan just took advantage of the situation to become somebody else and take off for parts unknown. But aren't Harvey's people looking for him?"

Trent glanced at Holly before he answered. "Well, here's the kicker. I wired Postmaster Case down in Council Hill yesterday afternoon, and he wired back that he knows this Harvey Stump. He is living in a house in Council Hill that he inherited from his parents, who both died of the influenza back in the fall. I wired him right back and asked Mr. Case if Harvey had changed into somebody else while he was in Europe, and he answered me that the Stumps had just moved to Council Hill a few months before they died, and nobody in town had ever seen Harvey until he got back from the war to claim his inheritance."

The color drained from Holly's face. "Oh, Lord! Are you saying that this Harvey Stump is really Dan?"

"I don't know, ma'am, but it's possible. Scott telephoned the county sheriff's office and they're sending out a deputy. Scott and the deputy from Muskogee will head down there tomorrow and go to the Stump house—see if the man living there is the lowlife scum who stole Harvey's life and did wrong by this lady."

Shaw had a couple of questions of his own. "Hang on, now. If Dan Johnson killed a fellow in a bar fight and deserted, why would he be so stupid as to head back toward Okmulgee, his hometown, in the first place? Any fool would know that's the first place the military police are going to look for him. Why not head for Canada or Mexico?"

Trent shrugged. "Who knows why anybody does anything? Could be he met Harvey somewhere betwixt Baltimore and Oklahoma, and Harvey told Dan about how his folks had died and now he was sole owner of their new house in Council Hill, where he had never even been. Maybe Dan devised a plan to do harm to Harvey and steal his life before they even got to Oklahoma. Could be it was just luck, if you can call it that, that Harvey died before Dan could dispatch him. Or maybe I'm dead wrong about the whole thing. After Scott goes down to Council Hill tomorrow and talks to whoever is living in Harvey Stump's house, we'll know better."

Holly scraped her chair back and left the kitchen in a hurry, fighting back tears. Alafair made a move to follow her but Shaw put a hand on her arm. "Let her be, honey. Even if the yahoo down in Council Hill is Dan Johnson, it's not her concern anymore."

Alafair looked at him with a mixture of surprise and disdain. "Maybe not. But that don't mean her heart isn't broke."

• • ● • •

Holly had no thought of what to do when she walked out of the house by way of the front porch. She simply could not stand the sympathetic looks she was getting from the people at the table. When she stepped out the door, all four of the family dogs stood up from their afternoon siesta on the porch, languidly performed a coordinated stretch, and ambled over in a friendly, wagging, slobbery pack to greet her.

She gave them each a head-pat and an ear scratch, grateful for their nonjudgmental affection. Shaw's two hunting hounds, Buttercup and Crook, went back to the corner to resume their nap, but the old shepherd Charlie Dog and the young mutt Bacon followed her down the steps and out the gate into the drive. She stood quietly for a long minute, gazing toward the woods behind the house, but not seeing.

She started walking, and before she knew it she had traversed the long drive. Bacon, the mutt, had lost interest and disappeared by the time she made it to the section line road, but Charlie Dog kept her company as she turned toward town.

Charlie Dog was old and fat and could only follow at a stately pace. But that was no problem since Holly's damaged feet began to protest long before she reached the highway, and the best she could do was limp along. When she finally reached the turn onto the wide, graded, dirt road that led to civilization, she could go no longer. She found a likely rock between the road and the drainage ditch and sat down. The persistent shepherd sat down next to her and leaned his furry bulk into her side. She put an arm over him, enjoying his warmth.

The weather had cleared, but the air was chilly and she had not thought to take her coat. Or thought of anything at all. She and the dog sat there for a quarter of an hour or so before a white delivery vehicle lumbered down the road from the north. It pulled to a stop beside her with a rattle and grinding of gears, and a pleasant-looking young man with unruly straw-colored hair sticking out from under his cap leaned out the window.

"Howdy, Miss, anything wrong?"

Holly gave him a thorough once-over before she replied. "Where are you headed?"

"Why, Miss, I'm hauling a load of screws and nails to Henryetta. You need a ride?"

"Is Henryetta anywhere near Council Hill?"

The driver grinned. "I'll be going through Council Hill on my way to Henryetta. If you're looking for a lift, jump right in and I'll drop you off."

Chapter Twelve

Gee Dub didn't finish dinner, either. He waited until everyone's attention was engaged elsewhere and slipped away from the table and out the back door. He hunted for Holly around the property for quite a while, but she was nowhere to be found. Finally he gave up and went back to the toolshed. Moretti was already there, sitting next to the Franklin stove, smoking a cigarette.

Gee Dub pulled up a chair. "When did you come in?"

"Just now. I nearly got my eyes pecked out by a mockingbird when I opened the door."

"Yeah, there's a pair building a nest under the eaves, here."

"You want me to climb up and get rid of it for you?"

Gee Dub was shocked by the suggestion. "Forget it, Private. Leave them alone. They're just trying to make a place to raise their family. Listen, before you came in, did you see a woman run out of the house?"

"No, I didn't see nobody. Hey, Lieutenant, you look like you've been sucking lemons. What's up?"

Moretti listened with interest as Gee Dub filled him in on the new developments in Holly's case. He threw his cigarette butt into the stove before he said, "Well, this is interesting. What do you expect she'll do now?"

"Nothing. What can she do?" Gee Dub got up and paced the room for a minute or two, then sat down on his bunk and drew one of the cartridge boxes out from under his pillow. He slid it open and retrieved the solitary cartridge.

"What's on your mind, Mr. Tucker?"

Moretti's voice startled Gee Dub out of his reverie, and he smiled. "Justice."

"You like her." It wasn't a question. "You think maybe she'd be grateful to you if you got rid of the rat."

"She was already rid of him. I doubt if she's the kind of woman who would subscribe to vengeance."

"Who knows what a woman thinks, Lieutenant? I've known some of them to be way more vengeful than any man. One thing, though. Is it her you want to avenge or is it those women in France you couldn't do anything for? Even if you could avenge the wrong done to Holly, that wouldn't cure what ails you."

"I don't think anything will cure what ails me, Moretti."

"You're too hard on yourself, Mr. Tucker. You saved my life a bunch of times before you got sent off to help the Limeys."

Gee Dub held up the bullet between his forefinger and thumb and regarded it thoughtfully. "If I was back in France and caught a soldier abusing a civilian, I'd have him up on charges faster than you could spit."

"What if it was a bunch of Fritzes?"

"I'd shoot them."

"You did shoot them, Lieutenant. You remember that?"

"Of course I do."

"Not all them were Germans, either."

Gee Dub leaned forward and placed his hands over his ears. "God Almighty," he murmured, not entirely blasphemously, "men are sorry creatures." He stood up. "Come on, Private. Let's you and me go for a ride."

Holly knew she must look as awful as she felt. When she walked into the Westlake Restaurant on Main Street in Council Hill, Oklahoma, the waitress took one look at her and hustled her to a table in the corner.

"Whatever happened to you, honey?" The woman's tone was full of concern. "Do you need some help, sugar? Is there anything I can do for you?"

Holly unconsciously raised a hand to her cheek. It was wet with tears. She wished the kind woman would leave her to her misery, but since it was obvious that was not going to happen, she said, "It's all right. I just found out that someone I cared for once has died. It took me aback, is all. I'd just like to sit here for a few minutes and get myself together, if that's all right."

The woman emitted a sympathetic cluck. "It sure is. I'm sorry to hear of your loss. You sit here a minute and I'll get you a drink of water." She hustled off, and Holly lowered her face into her hands.

It was all over at last, at least for her. She finally had enough money to go home, and that was what she intended to do. If it had been possible for her to leave Council Hill for Maine without going back through Boynton, she would have done it. She didn't much care about the few possessions in the carpetbag she had left at the Tucker farm. But the Tuckers had done so much to help her that it seemed to her like the height of ingratitude to leave without even a thank you. She would need to come up with a story to cover her sudden disappearance, though. She knew she wasn't going to alert the law about Dan. The wheels of justice would turn without any help from her.

The waitress set a tall glass of water on the table and Holly looked up. "When is the next train to Boynton, do you know?"

"Oh, the last train north left a couple of hours ago, Miss. Next one will be through tomorrow morning at seven. If you need a place to stay tonight, my sister sometimes takes in boarders. She keeps a nice clean place."

Holly sighed. The faster she could leave Council Hill, the better. It sounded like she'd be hitchhiking again. "Thank you, but that won't be necessary."

"You want something to eat? Might make you feel better."

Holly almost refused out of hand, but reconsidered. It had been hours since she had left the Tuckers' dinner table without eating, and she did feel a bit hollow. "I could eat a little something."

"My husband caught a big old catfish yesterday. I can fry you up a nice piece with some fresh cornbread."

Holly turned slightly green at the idea of more freshwater fish rolled in cornmeal and deep fried in bacon grease. "Maybe something lighter."

"I just baked a loaf of real wheat bread. Thank goodness the war is over and I can use as much wheat flour as I want! How about a couple slices, still hot from the oven, with some butter and honey."

"Perfect."

The waitress nodded and looked over Holly's shoulder at the front door. "I'll be right with you," she said, before disappearing into the kitchen.

Holly glanced behind her to see who had come in, expecting nothing. Her heart jumped when she recognized him. "Oh, my goodness. How did you find me this time?"

Gee Dub sat down and gave her an ironic smile before removing his black Stetson and hanging it on the back of his chair. "It didn't take a college degree to figure it out, Holly. Trent implies that Johnson could be living in Council Hill, and off you go."

"You're not my keeper, you know."

"Is that right? You could use a keeper. So you found him, did you? You were in his house for quite a spell. What did y'all have to say to one another?"

"You followed me?"

"Not exactly. It looks like you've been bawling again. Your eyes are all swollen. You are not a pretty cryer, I'm afraid."

"Gee Dub, Dan has changed. He knows he's been caught. When the sheriff comes, he's going to turn himself in without a fight."

His eyebrows lifted, as though he could not quite believe what he was hearing. "Oh, you think so, do you? Holly, Dan proved a long time ago that he'd do whatever he had to in order to weasel his way out of trouble. No, Dan is not going to turn himself in."

Holly grabbed his hand, and he winced. "Please don't inter-fere, Gee Dub. Please let it be. I don't have the strength to deal with it anymore. Let things turn out on their own now. I just want to forget all about it and go back to where I belong." She looked down at his hand, still clutched in hers. "What happened to your knuckles? They're all skinned."

Before he could respond, the waitress came out of the kitchen with a plate containing a fragrant pile of fresh bread covered with melting butter and honey. She gave Gee Dub a suspicious glare. "Is this man bothering you, dear?"

"No, it's all right. He's a friend."

"I'm here to take her home," Gee Dub said to the waitress. "But first, I'll take some of that good-smelling bread, if you don't mind." He watched the woman until she disappeared into the kitchen, then turned back to Holly. "Now, you and me need to get our stories straight."

Chapter Thirteen

After disappearing from the dinner table, Holly did not come back to the house again for the rest of the afternoon. Alafair tried not to worry about the poor girl. Considering her reaction in Okmulgee to finding out that her supposed husband was already married, Alafair figured Holly was one to try and run from her pain. She had left her belongings on the bed in the girls' room, so Alafair knew she couldn't get very far. She would show up eventually. Surely she would.

The children came home from school and Alafair put them to their chores. Charlie Dog padded into the house late in the afternoon and followed her around while she did housework. The business of living occupied Alafair's attention and she didn't have time to think about anything else—until Shaw came in for supper alone and it occurred to Alafair that she had not seen Gee Dub all day, either. Alafair turned around to look at Shaw, wiping her hands on her apron. Her brow was knit. "Gee Dub went off on his own again today?"

Shaw read her expression. "I expect. I haven't seen him since he slipped out of the house at dinner. Did Holly ever turn up?"

"No, I haven't seen her since dinner, either."

Shaw didn't like the implication, but he wasn't going to let Alafair know that. He walked over next to Alafair at the cabinet and nonchalantly picked up a biscuit off the serving platter. "Gee Dub doesn't tell me his plans these days. Maybe he finally went into Boynton to scare up a job of work for himself, or for Holly. Maybe they went off for a ride together. Don't worry, honey, they'll show up."

"I wish they would, and right quick." Alafair glanced behind her to make sure none of the children were within hearing distance. "Shaw, I'm worried about him. What if he's ridden to Okmulgee to confront Daniel Johnson before Scott and the deputy can get to him tomorrow? What if he's decided to take matters into his own hands and give Johnson a thumping?"

Shaw was not quite as alarmed at the prospect. "Well, Johnson could use a thumping. But that don't sound like something Gee Dub would do. Besides, Holly's well shet of him, so why would Gee Dub complicate things? He likely went out to sit on his hill."

"What if he does take a notion to beat up the man and Johnson presses charges? Shaw, he could end up in jail, or worse."

"Johnson, if it is him, doesn't know yet that he's been found out. Even if Gee did take a notion to ride six miles on horseback to give Dan Johnson a sock in the jaw for being a rat, Johnson would be so eager to keep his secret that he wouldn't do a thing."

"Dan Johnson killed somebody, Shaw. He might be so eager to keep his secret that he'd kill again."

Shaw had thought of that, but he said, "Alafair, the whole of the Kaiser's army couldn't kill our boy. He can take care of himself."

• • ● • •

But Gee Dub and Holly were not home for supper, or by bedtime, either. Neither Shaw or Alafair expressed their worry to the children, but the girls were expert readers of their parents' moods and knew better than to ask questions. Supper and the rest of the evening were quiet affairs. The girls were asleep and Shaw was preparing for bed, one leg out of his trousers, when Alafair, already in her nightgown and seated on the edge of their bed, finally broke the silence.

"Maybe they run off together."

Shaw paused in his disrobing, leg in the air, and gave his wife a narrow glance. "I reckon you'd like that."

"Better that than anything else I can conjure up."

"Alafair, you ain't going to be able to save the boy that way."

"What way?"

"Not every ill can be cured by the love of a good woman."

She shot him a look of mild insult and he laughed.

"Maybe not," she said. "But nothing makes a burden easier to bear like someone to share it with."

"Well, I do agree with that. Still, Gee Dub's mind is full of troubles and I think he ought to deal with them before he can deal with anything else."

"Now, I'd buy that argument, except for the fact that Gee Dub himself seems more interested in that gal than in his own tribulations."

"He just wants to be distracted by that pretty girl and not have to pull himself together."

His comment shocked her. She thought of her two sons who died in infancy. "Some trials are so grievous that you can't just 'pull yourself together,' Shaw. Maybe helping that poor girl is his way of helping himself."

Shaw had successfully removed his trousers and pulled his nightshirt over his head by this time. He sat down next to her and put an arm around her shoulders. "I know. I shouldn't have said that. That girl has troubles of her own. She's too apt to go off half-cocked. That's what got her in this pickle. Both those young people are suffering in their minds, but there isn't anything we can do to help them. I don't know that they can help each other, either. It's not like when our young'uns were little and we could kiss their skint knees and make it better. They're just going to have to figure it out themselves."

Alafair leaned into his side. "Still, we ought to go out looking for them first thing tomorrow."

"That was my plan," Shaw said.

● ● ● ● ●

Alafair did not sleep well. Night was nearly done but the old red cock had not yet crowed when Alafair was startled from her half-sleep by the creak of the front door opening. She was out of bed and in the parlor almost before she had time to think about it.

She could see a shadowy figure outlined against the lesser dark of the front window—a woman. She felt a brief pang of disappointment that it was not her son, quickly followed by the hope that Gee Dub had deposited Holly at the house and gone back to his own room.

Holly's voice came to her in a whisper out of the dark. "Mrs. Tucker? I'm so sorry…"

Alafair retrieved a fireplace match from the mantle over the stove and fumbled to light one of the kerosene lamps by feel. "Holly, sugar, where have you been? We've been worried sick. Where is Gee Dub?"

"He brought me back here. He's gone to his room."

The lamp flared to life and Alafair turned up the wick before she crossed the room and forced Holly down onto the settee. Shaw had shown up, Alafair didn't know when, and was standing over them, his hands on his hips and an expression of concern on his face.

"Mr. and Mrs. Tucker, I wish I had never come here. I wish I had never brought this trouble to you. You've been so kind and I don't deserve it…"

Alafair cut her off. "Holly, where have you been?"

Holly sighed hugely and leaned back into the settee. "I thought I had to know," she said, staring at the floor. "I had to know before the law got to him if the man in Council Hill was Dan. I wanted an explanation. I wanted to hear it from his own mouth why he did that to me."

Shaw was aghast. "You went down to Council Hill?"

"Well, I tried," Holly said to the floor. "I didn't even know where Council Hill is, just that it's south. I walked out to the main road yesterday and tried to hitch a ride. But nobody who came by was going that way." She straightened. Both Shaw and Alafair looked as though they wanted to jump down her throat and pull out the words. If only she were as eager to tell them what had happened as they were to hear about it. "I figured I'd walk it. I made it a mile or so, but my feet gave out. The blisters are still pretty raw." Holly looked away. "It hurt so much I nearly cried. I tried to walk back, but I could only make it a little ways at a time before I had to sit down on some likely stump and rest a bit."

Shaw was still looming over them, thrumming with anger and impatience. "Miz Thornberry, what you did was not only dumb as dirt. If you'd got down there and the man is Johnson, why, he could have killed you. He killed before. Even if he didn't hurt you, if he'd got a look at you and legged it out of there before the law picks him up today, it'd be your fault. Now, you let Miz Tucker fix you something to eat and get cleaned up. You sleep today and then we're going to figure out how to get you back to Maine where you belong."

Both women watched, subdued, as Shaw stomped off into the bedroom. Alafair could see three pairs of eyes peeking around the lintel of the girls' bedroom door. She made a shooing motion and the eyes disappeared. She turned back to Holly. "Where did Gee Dub find you? How did you get back here? Surely you didn't walk back on them feet, or hitchhike in the dark. There wouldn't be any traffic on that road at night."

"Well, I don't know exactly where I was. I was pretty lost. Gee Dub found me somehow and brought me back on that big red horse of his. He does that, you know. Keep showing up when I get lost. I guess he looked for me for a while after I ran off." Holly had gone back to staring at the floor. She hardly seemed interested in her own answer.

Alafair let out a sigh of relief. "So Gee Dub went on back to his room after he dropped you off at the house?"

"Yes, that's what he said. He said he wants to sleep. He scolded me about as bad as Mr. Tucker did."

"Well, never mind, baby. At least y'all are safe. Now come with me into the kitchen and I'll feed you something and get some more salve for them feet."

"That's all right, Mrs. Tucker. I kind of like the pain," Holly said.

Chapter Fourteen

By mid-morning the children were in school, Shaw was at work, and Alafair's troublesome guest was sound asleep and out from underfoot for the moment. Gee Dub did not show up for breakfast, but Alafair figured it was better to let him sleep. She washed the breakfast dishes, mopped the floors, made the beds, trimmed the wicks, and planted more lettuce.

She was checking her pantry for likely home-canned vegetables to serve for dinner when she heard the chug of an automobile coming up the drive from the road. She reached the front porch in time to see Scott pull up by the front gate. He was accompanied by a hard-looking middle-aged man whom Alafair did not know. Scott caught her eye and nodded a greeting. He didn't look happy. The two men walked across the flagstone path and up the front steps onto the porch, where Scott made the introductions. "Alafair, this is U.S. Marshal Amos Gundry. He came down from Muskogee this morning to go with me to Council Hill and talk to Harvey Stump."

"Marshal…" The way she spoke the word made it sound more like a question than a greeting. Apparently, the government was more interested in finding the elusive Dan Johnson than she had suspected.

The dark-eyed man removed his hat and gave her a terse nod. "Miz Tucker. I'm looking for G.W. Tucker."

Alafair felt the Earth sway under her feet, but her expression showed nothing but mild curiosity. "He is not to home at the moment. Can I help you?"

Scott's eyes narrowed. "Do you know where he is, Alafair?"

"Off about his own business, I expect."

"Was he home last night?"

Alafair did not hesitate. Something bad had happened, and until she knew what it was, she was going to cast her wing around her son, even if it meant telling a lie. "Why, of course he was. What is this about?"

Marshall Gundry said, "Miz Tucker, yesterday afternoon a tall, dark-haired man on a chestnut mare paid an unannounced call on Harvey Stump, who as it turns out is really Daniel Johnson. According to a neighbor lady, this man exchanged hot words with Mr. Stump-Johnson on his front porch."

Alafair realized that she was twisting the corner of her apron into a tight knot. She opened her hand and deliberately smoothed out the material. "Is that so? Well, as far as I know, my son was here all day yesterday."

The marshal's nose twitched with distaste. "Well, I don't have much use for any man who'd marry up with two women at the same time and then desert them both. But that don't change the fact that when Sheriff Tucker and me went to Council Hill this morning, we discovered Mr. Johnson shot clean dead. I'd like to have a word with G.W. about it."

A rush of blood to her head blinded Alafair for a second. She blinked rapidly to clear her sight. "Dead?"

"Yes, ma'am. Dead as Moses. We found him in his garage. He was getting ready to light out, it looked like. He had packed his clothes and there was bag of cash in the car. The neighbor lady says she saw Mr. Stump-Johnson alive after the dark-haired stranger left, but she heard a shot later that night. He was shot right through the heart at real close range. A large caliber bullet. Went straight through him and into the back wall. I dug it out. Looks like a steel-tipped thirty-aught-six. Rifle bullet. Dropped him like a rock. Whoever shot him socked him in the face beforehand, as well. It was an ugly, ugly thing."

Alafair could hardly breathe. "And you suspect Gee Dub? Why on Earth?"

"I understand that the man the neighbor saw fits the description of your son. That don't mean he's the killer, but he could have been the one who argued with the deceased. I understand he is...friendly with one of the women Mr. Johnson wronged."

Alafair looked at Scott, astounded at his betrayal. Who else could have made that connection and told Gundry about it? She turned back to the marshal. "Did anybody see what happened?"

"No, ma'am. The neighbor woman said when she heard a pop last night she didn't think nothing of it. Boys are always shooting rats and critters around there. She didn't hear no fight at that time, so it could be somebody surprised him."

Alafair grasped at the one bit of hopeful news in Gundry's tale. No one actually saw Johnson get killed. She drew a breath and said to Scott, "Surely you don't think Gee Dub could have shot a man in cold blood?"

"I think we need to speak to him, Alafair," Scott said. "So you have no idea where he is right now?"

"No. Maybe he went into town to wait for y'all to come back from Council Hill. If I know Gee Dub, he's probably at the jailhouse with Trent. Or maybe he's visiting one of his sisters." All she could think about now was getting rid of them until she could get to Gee Dub somehow and tell him to run.

Scott was eyeing her funny. Alafair didn't care. Scott was kin. He shouldn't be casting suspicion on his own family member. If he suggested they search for Gee Dub on the farm right now, she was prepared to demand they get a warrant. But he did not go that far.

"Well, then, I reckon me and Marshall Gundry will try to scare him up in town. When you see him, you tell him we're looking for him."

Alafair felt her shoulders sag. "I will, Scott. You can count on that."

• • ● • •

Once Scott's Paige was out of sight, Alafair made a beeline out
the back door, across the yard, and into the barn. Her knees
weakened with relief when she saw that Penny was in her stall.
Gee Dub was still here. She passed through the barn to the
toolshed out back and knocked before she opened the door of
the bunk room. He was not there, but she went inside anyway.

The room was neat. Almost sterile. Both cots were made up
with tight military precision. When had he purloined a second
set of sheets from her supply? Perhaps he thought bedclothes on
both cots made the room look more symmetrical. She crossed
directly over to the cot he had been sleeping in and lifted the
pillow. The ammunition boxes were still there, but now both
were empty. The lone cartridge was gone.

She found his rifle right where it ought to be, on the rack
above the door. It was a good place to keep a rifle, out of the reach
of curious children as well as women who were middle-sized at
best. She pulled a chair over from the table and climbed up on
it to haul the rifle down. She could usually tell by the smell and
the condition of the barrel whether a gun had been recently
fired, but the interior of Gee Dub's rifle barrel was shiny and
only smelled of gun oil. He had just cleaned it. She replaced it
on the rack and climbed down, unsure of whether she should
be disappointed or relieved.

She sat down on the bed and took a breath. Her boy. Her
eldest son, her beloved Gee Dub, born kind and good-natured,
sharp and funny and smarter than anyone else she knew. If
the devil threatened to end the world if she didn't choose her
favorite child, she would have to admit that, of all her darling
children, Gee Dub might be the one. And now what? What had
he become when she wasn't there to help him?

Alafair was still sitting on the edge of the cot, holding the
empty boxes in her lap, when Gee Dub returned to the bunk
room nearly an hour later.

He hesitated when he caught sight of Alafair. Had she seen Moretti? His expression grew wary when he noticed the boxes in his mother's lap. "What's up, Ma?"

"A while ago I had a visit from Scott and a U.S. marshal out of Muskogee."

"Ah." Gee Dub removed his hat and jacket and hung them on the peg before seating himself on the other cot.

"What happened to your hand, son?"

He glanced down at his skinned knuckles. "Had an accident. What did the marshal want?"

"He was looking for you."

His eyebrows peaked. "Was he?"

"Seems some unknown person killed Holly's pretend-husband last night in Council Hill. The neighbor woman mentioned a dark-haired stranger's recent visit and the marshal wanted to ask you if you knew anything about it."

Gee Dub seemed at a loss. He stood up. "Johnson is dead?"

"Killed by someone who was determined to make sure he was extra dead. The marshal said he was shot right through the heart at close range." She hesitated. "Gee Dub…"

He cut her off. "When did this happen?"

"Last evening sometime. Son, did you do this thing? Did you ride all the way to Council Hill last night and kill Daniel Johnson?"

Gee Dub blinked, and drew back. He looked surprised that she would ask him such a thing. But not shocked. He didn't answer.

Alafair felt tears start to her eyes. She had expected him to be mortally offended by her accusation, to scold her, storm out. Not stand there staring at her with an unreadable expression in his dark eyes.

"Why would you think so?" he finally said.

"You were gone all night." She stood and seized his arms. She would have gotten right into his face if she had been tall enough. "Gee Dub, did you go there? Holly told me you found her on the road to Council Hill and brought her home. And now Johnson's shot."

He gently lifted her hands off of him and backed away. He lowered his head and looked at her from under his eyelashes. "He was a poor specimen. Can't say I'm sorry he's dead." He was matter-of-fact.

Alafair's tears were flowing, now. She removed her handkerchief from her sleeve and dabbed her cheeks, but she didn't allow herself to break down. "Maybe the world is better off without his like, Gee Dub. But that ain't what concerns me right now. Tell me what happened."

Her eyes widened when he laughed. "Well, you see, Ma, that's just it. I can't tell you what happened." He looked down at his skinned knuckles. "Sometimes I get lost. Sometimes I get so mad I go blind and deaf."

"Oh, son. The young fellow I know could never do such a thing."

He made a dismissive noise. "That fellow was killed in the war, Ma. The one who came back did do such a thing. Many times." He put his arm around her shoulder, and was relieved that she didn't pull away. "Ma, Cousin Scott or somebody from the marshal's office will come back for me directly. It'd be better if I head on in to town and turn myself in."

"Gee Dub, when you were in France, you were a soldier and did what you had to do. That's a different thing from cold-blooded murder. And let me tell you something. You are my son and I'll do anything to keep you safe. If you killed that man, then he deserved it. If you killed him and can't even remember it, then you're wounded, and wounded in the service of your country, to boot. I'm not going to let anybody hurt you." She was aflame with purpose. "You go saddle that mare of yours. I'm going to make you up a poke of vittles and some supplies and you're going to take out. I've saved some money. You can have it. I'll find out what happened, son. But even if I don't, or even if it was you who did it, don't you come back here. Don't come back ever."

Gee Dub was unsure how to react. "That isn't justice, Ma."

"I don't care about justice. I care about you."

He blinked, taken aback by Alafair's extraordinary statement. "I don't know what scares me more…that I might hang or that my own ma doesn't care if I am a murderer. But I am not going to turn tail like a whipped cur. Besides, maybe it isn't as bad as you think. Maybe Scott just wants to question me."

"Gee Dub…"

"Where is Holly, Ma?'

She blinked at the unexpected question. "She's still asleep. You rode back here together. Can't Holly vouch for your whereabouts?"

"I didn't come across her on the road until early this morning. She doesn't know anything."

"Listen, son, don't turn yourself in."

"I'm not waiting until they hunt me down. Makes me look even more guilty."

"I'm not saying that. I'm saying don't turn yourself in today, at least. Wait until we know more about what happened."

He didn't respond. For a moment he gazed at her out of dark eyes that gave nothing away, then his lips turned up in half a smile. "Did the mockingbird dive at you when you came looking for me?"

Alafair's eyes widened. "What? No, I didn't see any bird."

No, Gee Dub wouldn't think so. The mother bird recognized a kindred spirit when she saw one.

• • ● • •

Alafair's plan was to make Gee Dub swear to stay in his room until she had a chance to find Shaw in the field and bring him home. Between the two of them, she was certain that they could come up with a plan to get Gee Dub out of harm's way. She did not doubt that Shaw would feel the same as she did, no matter what odd notions of duty over family that Gee Dub had picked up in Europe.

She didn't get the chance to find out. She had just headed back to the house to fetch her coat and warn Holly when she was met on the path. Scott had gotten rid of Gundry somehow and come back to the farm as quickly as he could.

They both stopped in the middle of the path and eyed one another warily.

"Where is he, Alafair?"

"He isn't here, Scott."

"Alafair, I just talked to Miz Thornberry up to the house and she told me that he found her on the road to Council Hill and brought her home this morning."

"That don't prove that he went to Council Hill. He went looking for Holly. He's got tender feelings for that gal, you know that." She was thinking fast, now. "Maybe she did get to Council Hill after all, Scott, and Gee Dub came across her on her way back here." Alafair liked Holly, but she wouldn't hesitate to divert suspicion to her for Gee Dub's sake.

The comment almost made Scott smile. If one of his own boys were in this situation, he was quite sure his wife, Hattie, would throw anyone on Earth to the wolves if she thought it would protect him. "Alafair, I just want to talk to him. Gee Dub can speak for himself."

"He didn't do it, Scott, you know that. Besides, I can't let you go hunting around here on the farm without you have a warrant."

"Where is Shaw?'

Alafair bit her lip, full of resentment. Scott intended to play his trump card. Man over woman. She did not appreciate his trying to put her in her place. "It's the middle of the day. He's out in the field somewhere."

"Well, I'll just have a talk with him…" He bit off his sentence and looked past her, an expression of surprise on his face.

She did not need to turn around to know that Gee Dub had come out of the toolshed and was walking toward them. They had been standing close enough to the back window of the shed for him to hear what was going on.

Alafair begged Scott to wait to take him until they could find Shaw. Anything to delay the inevitable. But Gee Dub nixed that idea. "Let's get it over with," he said.

The three of them walked back to the house together and Alafair watched from the drive as Gee Dub climbed into the Paige next to Scott and they drove away without a backward glance. She felt unreasonable anger at Holly for innocently telling Scott that Gee Dub was here, and unreasonable anger at Gee Dub for turning himself in without a by-your-leave. As for Scott, she wondered if she would ever be able to forgive him.

But she burned with hatred for the late Daniel Johnson. Whoever killed the despicable piece of garbage was doing God's work. And yet, if she was going to save her son, Alafair was going to have to find out who the killer was before the law did. Because if it was Gee Dub after all, she would try to find some way to destroy the evidence. She turned back toward the bunk room, determined to hide Gee Dub's rifle in the hayloft.

Chapter Fifteen

March 1919

Gee Dub thought that being in jail wasn't bad at all. He had a warm bed and three squares a day and didn't have to think about anything. It was rather nice to sit there and stare at the wall and wait for events to unfold without his having to do anything. The cold snap of the previous week was over and there was a definite feeling of spring in the air. The wind had changed direction and a fresh, warm breeze was wafting in through the open window above his cell.

Of course it didn't hurt that the jailers were his father's cousin Scott and his soon-to-be brother-in-law Trent Calder. Since three of his sisters lived in town, he could count on a parade of comforts throughout the day. Alice brought him fresh biscuits for breakfast and a lavender-scented quilt and down pillow. When Ruth came by at noon with a sumptuous repast in a basket for dinner, Trent unlocked the cell and the three of them ate fried chicken, cornbread, and cream pie around Trent's desk in the front office. Martha and her husband, Streeter, dropped in around suppertime with rice and ham gravy and more pie and sat with him in his cell to eat and talk about topics unrelated to Gee Dub's situation. Major Streeter McCoy had not yet been mustered out of the Army, but he had been transferred from

Washington City to Oklahoma City a couple of months earlier, so he did manage to get home most weekends.

All in all, it was pleasant, at the moment at least, and Gee Dub determined he was going to enjoy it while he could. Scott had told him that Marshal Amos Gundry planned to come back to Boynton on the afternoon train tomorrow, when Gee Dub would be transferred into his custody for the trip back to Muskogee. Gee Dub wasn't looking forward to riding the train while handcuffed to a marshal, but he tried not to think about that right now.

Martha and Streeter were still sitting in the cell with him when Alafair and Shaw showed up and brought the children with them. The cell and the hallway were crammed with his relations, all asking him questions and giving him advice. He tried to remain civil, for the children's sake. His nine-year-old cousin Chase Kemp seemed delighted to be related to an outlaw, but Gee Dub's three youngest sisters were distressed to see him in jail.

The crowd of people in the confined space reminded him too much of the trenches. He could tell that his mother was aware of his discomfort and he gave her a pleading look.

"Come on, then, you lot," Alafair said. "Y'all are sucking up all the air in here and Gee Dub is about to smother."

Martha and Streeter ushered the children out, leaving the parents to say goodnight.

"Mama and me will be back first thing tomorrow, son," Shaw said, "and Lawyer Meriwether will be with us."

Gee Dub responded with an absent nod and turned to Alafair. "Why didn't Holly come, Ma? Is she still at the house?"

Alafair and Shaw exchanged a glance. "She said she didn't want to impose on the family visit, son. She wants you to know she's thinking of you and that she'll see you tomorrow morning before the marshal gets here."

"Take care of Holly, Mama. Don't blame her for any of this. It's none of it her fault."

Trent gently maneuvered Shaw and Alafair out of the cell and locked the door behind them. Alafair turned and gripped the bars. "Son, we'll talk in the morning. You listen to me, Gee Dub, we'll figure this out, don't you worry."

● ● **●** ● ●

Trent saw the jailhouse visitors out, leaving the door between the cells and the office open. As soon as the crowd of Tuckers left the room, Moretti slipped in behind them and leaned against the wall.

Gee Dub came up off his cot like a shot and would have burst through the bars if he had been able. "Private, where in hell have you been?" Before Moretti could answer, Gee Dub spent a few moments exhausting the colorful new vocabulary he had picked up in France. When he wound down, Moretti removed his flat cap.

"Sorry, Lieutenant," he said, careful not to get within grab-bing distance. "I figured I can't stay out at your folks' farm anymore, so I moved into town. I've been waiting out front for your family to leave before I came in to see you. There sure are a lot of them!"

"Do you know what happened down in Council Hill?"

"Of course I do, Mr. Tucker. I was right there with you, remember?

"Did you kill that man, Moretti? Tell me."

Moretti's blinked. "You've been having those blackouts again? I thought you were rid of those."

Gee Dub took a breath and lowered himself onto the cot. "I thought so too. I was doing better after I got back to the States. If I had any blackouts while I was at Fort Benning before I got mustered out, I wasn't aware of it and nobody told me about it."

Now that he was not in immediate danger of being strangled, Moretti moved up closer to the bars. "None of those boys down in Georgia were apt to get shot any minute. Nor you, either."

Gee Dub clicked his tongue. "I hate to think I need Army life in order to be sane; somebody telling me where to be and knowing what I'm supposed to do every minute. Seems like since

I got home I'm either off in a fantasy or on war footing. And since Holly talked to that rat bastard, I've been worse than ever."

"Mr. Tucker, maybe you'd better tell the sheriff everything."

"Not unless I have to. If I can keep her name out of it, if I can wiggle around this, that's what I'll do."

"You want me to talk to your family?"

"Hell, no, not yet. That's just one more thing I'd have to deal with, and to no good end."

"You'll never be convicted of murder if I have anything to say about it, sir."

Gee Dub gave his young visitor a speculative once-over. "Are you going to confess?" His voice was heavy with irony.

Moretti laughed. "Well, I hope it doesn't come to that, sir. I will go with you on the train to Muskogee, though, if you want me to."

"I doubt if the marshal will let me bring my retinue along on the trip."

"I'll be discreet, Lieutenant. I'll sit behind him. He won't even know I'm there."

• • ● • •

Holly had no choice but to go with the family to see Gee Dub off. With her injured feet, there was no other way she could get to town. She rode in the back of a hay wagon, seated on old quilts along with the three youngest Tucker girls. The sun had barely cleared the horizon when they left the house.

When they got to town, they found that the rest of the clan had arrived before them. The five grown daughters, the odd son-in-law, the nephew, and various grandchildren were milling around on the boardwalk when Shaw pulled up in front of the jailhouse.

"Scott won't let us in, Daddy." Martha McCoy was indignant. "He said we had to wait for y'all."

Shaw handed the reins to Alafair and climbed down from the driver's seat. "I don't blame him, honey. When the marshal gets here he's going to think we're staging a jailbreak as it is. Y'all wait here while I find out what's going on."

Alafair and the girls dismounted from the wagon when Shaw went inside, but Holly stayed seated, apart from the chattering activity on the sidewalk, wishing she were away from here and yet desperate to figure out a way to speak to Gee Dub alone before the marshal took him away. Her problem was solved for her when Shaw reappeared.

"Scott says we can go in and talk to Gee one and two at a time, but we can't all go in at once. Holly, Gee Dub wants to see you first, since you didn't come with us yesterday."

• ● ● ● •

Gee Dub got right to the point. "Are you going to stick around until this thing is resolved, Holly?"

She was standing a few feet back from the bars. It was as close as Scott would let her approach Gee Dub's cell. Her plan to speak to him on her own was thwarted by Scott's presence. He clearly had no intention of allowing any collusion. Holly blinked at Gee Dub's blunt question. "Of course I am."

His dark-eyed gaze was riveted on her face. "I'd just as soon you didn't. There is no reason in the world for you to get any more mixed up in this than you have already. I wish you'd let me give you some money so you could get out of Oklahoma."

Holly shot a glance at Scott, standing at her shoulder. He did not look back. He simply gazed into space with crossed arms and a stolid expression. "I imagine I will probably be called as a witness, Gee Dub," she said. "Besides, I want to do whatever I can to help."

His fingers curled around the bars. "You just remember what we talked about."

Scott did not let that comment pass. "Wait a minute…"

Gee Dub hastened to reassure him. "Nothing sinister, Scott. I want her to go home, is all. I told her she don't belong here." He looked back at Holly. "I'm not kidding, now. You promised me, remember?"

Holly found herself blinking away tears. "I remember what we talked about. Please don't worry about me, Gee Dub. Please don't worry."

● ● ● ● ●

After Holly left, a mere quarter hour passed before Scott came back into the cell room. He closed the door to the outer office and approached Gee Dub's cell. Gee Dub took a step back, not afraid of Scott, but not eager to face whatever was coming next.

"Gundry's here," Scott said.

Gee Dub nodded, resigned, and leaned over to pick up his jacket off the cot.

Scott released an audible breath. "I don't know what kind of tale you and Miz Thornberry have cooked up between you, but I suggest you don't volunteer any more information without Lawyer Meriwether present. I do not want to turn you over to Gundry, Gee Dub. You are kin and it goes against the grain to serve you up like a nice steak. Besides, your ma can hardly bring herself to look at me as it is."

That made Gee Dub smile. "I appreciate it, Scott, but I don't hold it against you. You've got to do your job."

"Gee Dub, why are you protecting her?"

The question should not have been unexpected, but Gee Dub took a moment to reply. "What makes you think I'm protecting somebody?"

"'Cause I don't think you killed that man."

"That's good to hear. Do you have some reason for that opinion, other than confidence in my moral fiber?"

"You are acting mighty strange, boy. I'd think you'd be eager to defend yourself, but you're not talking. I've known you all your life and I know what kind of man you are. But you've been to war and that can change a man. Yes, you might have done it. But whoever killed Johnson shot him at real close range. Almost like he put the weapon right on the man's chest before he fired. You wouldn't have had to do it that way. You could have shot him from a mile away. I've seen you shoot, son. You don't miss."

Gee Dub did not respond, but he did not disagree, either. It wouldn't have done any good. Everyone in his family knew he was a prodigy when it came to firearms and always had been. In the Army he had made such high scores in marksmanship that he had been tapped to train recruits in riflery right out of Officer Candidate School.

"It is that gal, isn't it?" Scott said. "You're trying to protect Miz Thornberry. I can see that you're sweet on her. So what happened, Gee Dub? Was it her? Did she go to Council Hill that day? She could have killed him. Even a little critter like her, even somebody who had never shot a rifle could have put a gun to his heart and pulled the trigger."

Gee Dub knew that Scott was goading him. "Look, Scott, that isn't going to work. Holly didn't kill anybody. Where would she get a rifle, anyway?"

"Maybe it was Johnson's rifle and she took it with her after she shot him. By the way, you own a Springfield. I remember when your daddy bought it for you. I asked Shaw to bring it in and save me having to get a warrant to search the farm, but he says he can't find it. Where'd you stash it, Gee Dub? I'd just as soon not tear through Shaw's place trying to find it."

"I didn't stash it anywhere," Gee Dub said. "It ought to be on the rack above the door in my room, where it always is. Dad knows where I keep it."

"You think Shaw just don't want to turn it in? That doesn't sound like him."

Gee Dub made a sound that could have been taken for an ironic laugh. "Dad wouldn't. If I were you I'd ask Mama about it."

The idea of confronting Alafair made Scott grimace. "Why in blazes don't you just tell me what happened?"

"I don't know who killed Johnson, Scott, I promise."

Scott's voice dripped with frustration. "I think you know a lot more than you're telling."

Now Gee Dub did laugh. "Now, that's where you're wrong, Scott."

• • ● • •

Only Scott Tucker, Alafair, Shaw, and Lawyer Meriwether accompanied Gundry as he walked his handcuffed prisoner to the railway station. Scott had had to negotiate with Marshal Gundry even for that small concession. Gundry was wary of anyone who might be tempted to slip a file or a derringer into a felon's pocket while he wasn't looking. Even though Scott had warned them to keep their distance, the rest of the family trailed along behind. Gundry kept glancing over his shoulder as though they were a mob ready to bonk him on the head and flee up into the hills with his prisoner. Alafair couldn't help but reflect that if the extended Tucker family had never moved to Oklahoma, if they still lived in the Ozarks where she was born, that is exactly what would probably happen. Sometimes living in civilization and adhering to the rule of law had its disadvantages.

As for Gee Dub, he would have preferred that no one in his family had come to town to watch him be taken away. He almost asked his parents to stay at the jailhouse with his siblings, but he didn't have the heart. He decided he could put up with a little humiliation for his mother's sake. Scott had discreetly draped Gee Dub's jacket over the handcuffs that bound his wrists, so he wouldn't look quite so blatantly like a prisoner being escorted to his doom. Only Lawyer Meriwether had much to say as the group trudged the three blocks from the jailhouse to the train station, cautioning Gee Dub to keep his mouth shut and not volunteer any information without Meriwether present. Not that that was necessary. No one could keep his mouth shut better than Gee Dub Tucker.

Gundry did not allow Gee Dub's parents to hug him before they mounted the steps to the platform. The best they could do was hold his gaze till the last minute and promise to visit him as soon as possible.

Gee Dub was almost amused when Gundry searched him again as soon as they got into the rail car. "Cautious, aren't you, Marshal?"

Gundry didn't blink. "You got too many folks to keep an eye on every minute, Tucker. Can't be too careful."

They walked up the aisle to the middle of the car and Gundry directed Gee Dub into a seat next to the window, away from the platform so he could not see his family. Still, Gee Dub gazed out the window across the field of yellow grass next to the tracks. Green shoots were beginning to pop up between the weeds. He could see a few buildings in the distance and studied them for a long moment. The Pure Oil pumping station, a garage, a house. They were likely the last sight of Boynton he was going to have for the foreseeable future. He must have slipped out of time for a while, for when the train jerked and began to move, he was startled. He blinked and turned to orient himself to reality again. Gundry was watching him, eagle-eyed. The man in the seat facing them was occupied with a newspaper. Two women down the aisle, a mother and daughter, were talking to one another animatedly. Sitting across from the women, a dark-haired young man in a flat cap caught his eye. Private Moretti winked at him.

Chapter Sixteen

Holly was left sitting on a hard wooden chair under the front window of the jailhouse. Trenton Calder had been charged with minding the office, and, Holly suspected, with preventing her from running away. If that was Scott's reasoning, she didn't blame him. She had proved herself to be a flight risk. Trent had spent the night on a cot in the cell next to Gee Dub, and his startlingly red hair was still sticking up every which way. After the parade of Tuckers had left the office, Trent made coffee and offered to walk over to the bakery and buy a couple of fresh buns for Holly and himself. Alafair had fed her biscuits and bacon before they left the farm at dawn, but nerves made her hungry, so Holly accepted, and the two of them sat on either side of Trent's desk to nibble buns and drink coffee. Holly was aware that Trent kept eyeing her with a decidedly bemused look on his freckled face.

"You sorry you ever left Maine?" he wondered.

"Yes." Her tone indicated that she considered it a stupid question. She changed the subject. "So when is the big day that you are marrying Gee Dub's sister? It's Ruth, isn't it?"

Trent lit up with unstudied delight. "That's right. Ruth. April 27 is the day, one week after Easter Sunday."

"Which one is Ruth? Have I met her? Where does she live?"

"She was just here with her sisters, but I don't believe you've formally made one another's acquaintance yet. She lives just north of town with Miz Beckie MacKenzie, who is her old music teacher. Ruth has taken over Miz Beckie's students, and just between you and me, she has kindly taken over Miz Beckie, too. Miz Beckie's grandson was bad hurt in the war and she's taking it hard."

"Just how many sisters does Gee Dub have? I keep meeting people and hearing names and seeing little grandchildren flit in and out, but I haven't been able to keep a count."

"There're eight girls in that family, four of them married— soon to be five. Only two boys, Gee Dub and Charlie, who is still in the service."

"I understand you are just back from the service yourself."

"I am. I was in the U.S. Navy for the duration. Didn't cotton to it much."

"So you've come home to Boynton to marry and be town deputy."

Trent glanced away before he answered. "Well, what Scott wants is to retire from law enforcement and have me take over as the town sheriff. But Boynton don't pay enough to support a family on, so I reckon I'll be looking for another line of work as soon as Scott can rustle up a replacement for me."

"Do you have an occupation in mind?"

"I might apply to work with the Muskogee Police Depart- ment." He hesitated, then blurted, "Don't tell Miz Tucker yet."

Holly laughed. The image of tall, robust Trenton Calder quailing before matronly Alafair Tucker amused her. "Why, Mr. Calder, are you afraid to tell Mrs. Tucker that you intend to take Ruth to live in faraway Muskogee?"

"Nothing is decided on. I've been talking to Ruth about it. She's not keen to leave her family or Miz Beckie, either, but she understands that I can't just be Scott's dog's body for the rest of my life. Tell the truth, with all the boys coming back from the war, it's not that easy to find a good job these days. The Muskogee Police Department might not be in the market for anybody new." Trent bit into the soft bun, quiet for a moment. "Tell me, Miz Thornberry, have you decided what you're going to do with yourself, now that you're…umm…a free woman?"

She shrugged. "I really want to go home, Mr. Calder. Another thing that is sure, I intend to learn to curb my impulses. If I spent as much time planning my future as I do firing off like a cannon, I might be able to make something of myself."

"Please call me Trent, Miz Thornberry. I have a few years left before I have to answer to Mr. Calder. I'm sorry to hear that you don't take to this country. I figured you might be staying on. Maybe I was mistook, but I got the feeling at dinner the other day that there was a spark between you and Gee Dub."

Holly's cheeks reddened, but she cultivated a look of indifference. "He's a nice man and I will do anything I can to help him. He helped me when I needed it. But we are far too different. And I don't see myself living here for the rest of my life. I do not belong here, that is for sure."

• • ● • •

After the train taking Gee Dub to Muskogee pulled out of the station, Alafair and Shaw retrieved Holly from the jailhouse and gathered with the rest of the family at Alice Kelley's white-frame house on Second Street in order to devise a plan of action. Their son and brother had been arrested on suspicion of murder and none of them were going to let that stand, if they could help it.

Holly did not want to be included in the planning session, but her wishes had no bearing. It was because of her that Gee Dub was in this situation. None of the Tuckers seemed to blame her, but she blamed herself. She was in it up to her neck and she was not going anywhere until Gee Dub was free and justice was done.

Holly couldn't decide whether to be grateful for the open-hearted way she had been taken in by this generous clan, or to curse the day that Gee Dub Tucker had ridden up to her in the middle of a muddy field. One thing she could say with certainty was that she had no idea how she had gotten sucked into these people's lives nor how she was going to get out. At the moment, she was overwhelmed and disoriented.

There were so many Tuckers! She was aware that Shaw and Alafair had ten children, many of whom had spouses and children of their own. But knowing it and seeing what that actually meant were entirely different things. The Kelleys' parlor was stuffed with people sitting on every flat surface as well as the floor. So many bodies made the room seem hot and airless. Holly was crammed into a corner at the back, near the French doors that led to the dining room. The three youngest Tucker girls, Blanche, Sophronia, and tooth-deprived Grace, had all taken a shine to their exotic visitor and were arrayed on the floor at her feet. Holly thought she might be able to figure out the names of Alafair and Shaw's actual offspring. The brunette by the front door, sitting with a sandy-haired man in uniform, was Martha, Alafair's look-alike eldest. Mary Lucas was the tall blonde next to the even taller and blonder Alice Kelley. Holly had already met little auburn-haired Phoebe, who was holding the infant George H. Day in her lap. Ruth was the one with reddish curls who was getting married to Deputy Trent Calder in April. The two sons were not there, but sons-in-law abounded—four in all, if you counted Trent. The missing one was Mary's husband, Kurt, still in serving his country back east. There was no way Holly could keep the babbling crew of grandchildren straight, so she didn't try.

Shaw was standing by the open front door, where he could be seen by everyone in the room. "I talked to Gee Dub in private this morning," he said. "He says that it wasn't him who killed Johnson, and of course I believe him. Now, I do think he knows more than he's telling, because he's been mighty sparse with the details. Why that is, I cannot say, but I expect it has something to do with Miz Thornberry, there."

Dozens of heads swiveled in Holly's direction, and her cheeks began to burn. "You think he's protecting me? I swear on all that is holy that I didn't kill Dan."

"No one said you did, darlin'." Shaw's tone was mild. "But Gee Dub may have seen something or made up a story in his mind that makes him think you are in danger. I don't know." He turned to address his remarks to the general audience. "As y'all know, I have retained Lawyer Abner Meriwether on Gee Dub's behalf. Mr. Meriwether tells me he'll employ all means to get Gee off. He expects that even in the worst case, if Gee Dub is arraigned, he'll be able to get the charges reduced to voluntary manslaughter. He is not sure if he'll be able to get Gee Dub released on bail, but we'll see. Scott said that Johnson's parents and his legal wife in Okmulgee have asked to have the body released to them. They intend to go ahead and bury him in the family plot, after all."

Alafair straightened. "Now, that's odd. A few months ago when they thought the body that was found beside the road was their son, they refused to have anything to do with it. They told Scott to just bury him in a pauper's grave. Now they want to claim the body? What has changed?"

Shaw lifted a shoulder. "They're feeling guilty, I expect. They've had a lot of time to reconsider the coldhearted way they reacted the first time they heard their scoundrel of a son had met his maker. It's not often you get a chance to remedy your mistakes, and I'm not surprised they're taking the opportunity to do just that."

Alice spoke up. "Daddy, we ought to take turns going to Muskogee to see Gee Dub every day until he gets released."

"Mama," Mary said, "if you and Daddy want to go to Muskogee and stay with Aunt Sula so you can be close at hand, the girls can come stay with me and Chase and Judy."

Martha got to the point. "The question is, now that Gee Dub has been arrested, is Marshal Gundry going to keep investigating the murder or is he satisfied that he's got his man?"

The sandy-haired man next to her, her husband Streeter McCoy, said, "Honey, U.S. marshals don't do investigating. They just hunt people down."

"What about Scott?" Ruth wondered.

"Scott has no jurisdiction outside of Boynton," Shaw said.

Twelve-year-old Sophronia was aghast. "Are y'all saying that we're not going to do anything? That we're just going to let Gee Dub go to prison?"

"We're not going to let that happen, sugar," Shaw assured her.

"Well, what are we going to do, Daddy?" Sophronia's voice rose an octave.

Alafair had been listening to the conversation with a thoughtful look on her face. "I have an idea," she said.

Part II

Chapter Seventeen

Charles Tucker was the eldest son in his family, two years older than his brother, Shaw. He was by far the most financially successful of all his Tucker siblings, the owner of a busy sawmill and a large cotton farm just east of Okmulgee, Oklahoma's fourth-largest town at over seventeen thousand souls. The war had been good to Charles and his wife, Lavinia, what with the U.S. Government building military installations right and left and the price of cotton through the roof. Prices were still artificially high, even four months after the end of the war. But Charles had not gotten where he was by being a fool, so he was already planning to scale back cotton production and broaden his business interests in 1920.

Charles and Lavinia both looked as prosperous as they were, well padded in all the right places, expansive and welcoming. Lavinia was a busy, perky woman in her late forties with prematurely silvery-gray hair and a youthfully round face, sweet and untroubled. She loved hats and accessories, gloves, handbags, and scarves, and always dressed like she was going to tea with Queen Mary. Charles was tall, like all the Tucker men, with close-cropped black hair that was graying at the temples in a most distinguished fashion. Like his brother Shaw, Charles still sported an impressive mustache, even though facial hair was fast falling out of fashion, due to the popular aversion for anything reminiscent of Kaiser Bill. Shaw had even thought of shaving his off, but Alafair had talked him out of it. She didn't know if she'd recognize him without it.

When Alafair pulled her buggy to a halt in front of her in-laws' two-story brick house in the early afternoon, Charles was at work, but Lavinia gave her a warm welcome and settled her in the lush parlor with tea and little sandwiches. Before Alafair had a chance to explain her mission, Lavinia said, "What happened to the young lady who needed employment, Alafair? Charles still has an opening in the sawmill office, as long as she is aware that it would only be a short-term position."

It took a while for Alafair to relate every detail of what had happened over the past week. Lavinia was horrified. Her own son had come back from overseas with a bullet lodged in his thigh and a permanent limp. After vowing staunch familial support, financial and otherwise, Lavinia leaned back into her chair with a speculative look on her face. "Why do you suppose Mr. Johnson's abandoned first wife agreed to throw her faithless man a send-off? If my husband had done to me what he did to her, I reckon I'd tell the law to throw his carcass in a ditch somewhere."

Alafair shrugged. "It's probably the parents' idea. No matter what kind of a scoundrel he was, he was still their boy." She thought of Gee Dub and swallowed a lump in her throat. "On the other hand, maybe the wife figures she will have some inheritance coming."

"I don't see how. The property where Dan Johnson was living in Council Hill would have to go to the next of kin of the dead soldier whose life he stole, I'm sure."

"I'm told that poor Mr. Stump didn't have any family living, so who knows what will happen? That's not my lookout, anyway. I am only interested in finding out who sent the blackguard Dan Johnson to his eternal damnation and getting Gee Dub out of jail."

Lavinia liked the way she had put that, and smiled. "Do you know when the funeral is?"

"Not exactly. Scott only knows that they planned to bury him as soon as the body was released, and it has been. The coffin would have been shipped here on the train yesterday."

"Johnson is a pretty common name, but I'm not acquainted with anyone of that name. What do you know about the family? Do you know what church they go to?"

"I don't know much. Holly never mentioned a church home. She said that she thought the late Dan Johnson was a streetcar conductor. 'Course, she thought he was from Olathe, Kansas, too."

"Well, that's a hint, anyway. I'll ring up the streetcar terminal office. If Johnson was a conductor here in town, the folks he worked with will surely know something about the services." Lavinia clicked the receiver and asked the operator to connect her to the streetcar terminal. The man who answered the telephone at the terminal knew immediately what she was asking about. The resurrection followed by the instantaneous demise of his former colleague was big news.

Alafair watched anxiously as Lavinia listened to the voice on the other end, punctuating her silence with an occasional "Hmm," or "All right." After a perfunctory "Thank you," she replaced the earpiece in its cradle and turned toward Alafair.

"The funeral is day after tomorrow at the First Methodist Episcopal Church. The manager told me that the family is holding a reception at the home of Mr. Johnson's father after the burial. He said he expects a few of Johnson's fellow conductors will show up at the reception for the free grub."

"He said that?"

"He laughed, too. I reckon that neither one of Mr. Johnson's deaths caused much distress to the fellow who answered the phone, at least." Lavinia's expression showed that she relished this bit of information.

"Well! It'll be interesting to see if others of his acquaintance held Mr. Johnson in similar esteem," Alafair said. "Thank you, Lavinia. I aim to be at that funeral. I want to know why the Johnsons finally decided to give their son a send-off."

"Honey, I am not letting you go to that affair without me."

Chapter Eighteen

Holly did not like the idea of remaining at the Tucker farm longer than she already had, but she didn't know what else to do. Still, Alafair had gone to Okmulgee, Shaw was staying with his aunt in Muskogee in order to be close to Gee Dub, and the three youngest Tucker girls had moved in with their sister, Mary, while Alafair was away. Scott offered to give Holly a free room at the American Hotel, which was run by his wife, Hattie, but Holly didn't feel right about accepting charity from the lawman. He had been nothing but kind to her, but she suspected he still had his doubts about her involvement in a murder. Martha McCoy only had one bedroom in her apartment over the offices of the McCoy Land and Title Company. Phoebe Day had a tiny farmhouse and three tiny children. Ruth Tucker lived in a big house with many bedrooms, but it wasn't hers to offer. But Alice Kelley had an extra bedroom, an accommodating husband, and only one cheerful two-year-old to manage, so she was happy to invite Holly to be her guest.

Holly liked Alice. She was a tall, pretty, pale blonde who dressed like an illustration in a fashion magazine. She was also refreshingly blunt and impossible to insult. Her husband, Walter, was friendly to the point of being a flirt, but since he behaved this way right in front of his wife, Holly figured it was just his manner. Alice didn't seem bothered by it. Their little girl, Linda, was delightful—dark-eyed and dark-haired like her father, but her willful yet good-natured manner was her mother all over.

On the day after Alafair left for Okmulgee, Alice, with Linda in tow, drove Walter's Model T out to the farm to ferry Holly and her few belongings into town. Holly threw her carpetbag into the back and settled into the shotgun seat. Linda climbed into her lap like it was her due. The trip to Boynton over the unpaved roads was dirty, jostling, and noisy, but that didn't keep Alice from chatting nonstop as she drove. Later, Holly could not remember one thing Alice said to her, just that none of it had to do with the murder or with Holly's dilemma. In fact, the whole conversation was blessedly one-sided and Holly was able to listen with one ear, not think much, and enjoy the warm feel of the little girl in her lap.

When they reached Boynton, Alice pulled the auto into an open bay at the S.B. Turner Livery and Garage at the end of the main street into town. They were met by a man of some years who, despite his bright hazel-green eyes, was obviously Indian. Holly slid out of her seat with Linda in her arms.

"Good morning, Mr. Turner," Alice said. "How are you today?"

The little man greeted her with a wide smile. "I'm just fine, Alice. How are y'all?"

"Well as can be expected, Mr. Turner. I was wondering if you would give the auto a going-over? We'll be using it to drive to Muskogee directly."

The smile disappeared. "Well, sure, honey. I was mighty sorry to hear about Gee Dub's troubles. How is that going?"

"The hearing is tomorrow. Daddy has been in Muskogee ever since they arrested Gee Dub. Mama's in Okmulgee right now, trying to find some evidence that'll clear him. Even if he has to go to trial, Mr. Meriwether is pretty sure the judge will set bail. I don't know if he'll be able to come home then, or if he'll have to stay in Muskogee. I'll have to ask Walter how it works."

Mr. Turner extended a hand across the hood to Holly. "Are you the young lady who has caused all this trouble?"

The old man smiled when he said it and his tone was perfectly pleasant, but Holly was shocked that he would say such a thing to her. She managed to eke out an incoherent noise, but Alice came to her rescue before she had to think of a response.

"This is Miz Holly Thornberry, Mr. Turner. She traveled all the way down here from Maine looking for her husband."

Turner nodded. "Stories galore are flying around town about what happened. Folks are saying that Gee Dub came back from the war a changed man. That he beat that feller down in Council Hill to death with his bare fists for what he did to Miz Thornberry. Or that he rode down to Council Hill and shot the man's head clean off."

Alice's expression hardened. "Mr. Turner, Gee Dub hasn't even been charged with anything yet. It's just a coincidence that he was in Council Hill at all on the day Mr. Johnson was killed. Believe me, what I hear of Johnson, he was the kind of man who would have had folks lining up to shoot him. I don't appreciate whoever is spreading gossip about my brother, so don't you listen to them. Near to everyone in this town has known Gee Dub since he was born, and I can't imagine that one single person could ever think he'd kill somebody like that."

S.B. Turner was not as chastened by Alice's scolding as she might have hoped. "Honey, you know my boy Johnny was over there in Europe, too, and if Gee Dub lived through half the horrors that Johnny described to me and his ma after he came back, well, that would make a killer out of anybody."

"Not Gee Dub." Alice's expression said that was all there was to it.

S.B. nodded. There was no point in arguing. "If the lad does get indicted, I reckon half the town will head over to Muskogee to attend the trial. Like you said, Gee Dub is one of ours, and folks stand by their own."

"I appreciate that, Mr. Turner."

S.B. turned his attention to Holly in an attempt to lure her into the conversation. "I hear that your man stole another fellow's identification papers and commenced to living his life."

Holly shifted Linda to her other hip. "That seems to be what happened." She had no desire to expound.

"Maybe they traded papers," S.B. speculated. "Maybe they both thought to exchange lives."

"Considering that Johnson was wanted for manslaughter and on the run, that wouldn't be much of a trade for Mr. Stump," Alice pointed out.

S.B. was enjoying the topic of conversation far too much. "So it's true that the dead soldier Clell Rogers found by the side of the road back in December was the one whose life got stole?"

Holly could practically see the wheels turning in Mr. Turner's head as he stored each little bit of information they gave him for later distribution to the citizens of Boynton.

Alice seemed eager to set the record straight rather than let the local gossip mill churn out its own story. "That's him. Name of Harvey Stump. The poor fellow had inherited some property down in Council Hill, but he didn't have any family still living after he got out of the service. Nobody reported him missing."

"So where was this Dan Johnson from before he decided to go down to Council Hill and become Mr. Stump?"

"He was born and raised in Okmulgee," Alice said. "His folks still live there. They thought, along with everybody else, that he was dead, and here he was living not thirty miles away from them."

Mr. Turner's expression had changed while Alice was talking. "He was headed to Okmulgee?"

"That's right."

"And this was in December?"

Both Alice and Holly noticed the difference in Turner's tone and exchanged a glance. Alice said, "Mid-December, I think. I don't know the exact date, Mr. Turner, but Scott would. Why?"

Turner held up a finger to pause the conversation. He rummaged through a stack of papers on the makeshift desk beside the open garage door, came up with a ledger, and thumbed through it. He was running his index finger down a page when he said, "There was a fellow came through here on December 15th last year who rented a horse. He said he just needed it for two days to look at some property out in the country up around the Boynton Pool. Gave his name as Will Callahan. He paid ahead of time with cash money and left a big deposit on the horse, to boot, but he never came back. I reported the horse and tack stolen, and Scott wired most of the law around here to be on the lookout. It was near to two weeks before they found that horse in Okmulgee. The thief had sold it to somebody who didn't much care if the man he bought it off actually owned it. A sharp-eyed policeman saw the mare tied up outside a roadhouse and recognized the brand. I sure was glad to get that nag back. She's a good one, worth a lot of money."

"Did they find out what happened to the thief?"

"Naw. He just disappeared, and as long as I got Belle back, I didn't care to pursue it."

"Mr. Turner, was this man who rented the horse a soldier?" Holly said.

Turner seemed surprised to hear her speak. "Well, he wasn't in uniform. Had on a gray vest and a white shirt. Not very tall. Dark hair."

Holly removed the photo case from her handbag and held it out for Turner's inspection. "Is this him?"

Turner took the picture from her and scrutinized it closely. "Well, my word! I do believe that it is."

"Mr. Turner," Alice said, "you'd better tell Scott about this."

Scott looked up from Mr. Turner's ledger at the three people standing in front of him. "I had forgot about that stolen horse, S.B., but I should have put two and two together. I do remember that the fellow in Okmulgee who bought your mare said that he got her from a man at the very roadhouse where the police spotted her. He couldn't say more than that the man was young and called himself Will, but it looks like Will Callahan is really our Daniel Johnson. And if that is so, then instead of renting two horses or a buggy and going back to retrieve his ailing partner, Johnson lit out and left him to die beside the road. So Johnson went from here to Okmulgee before he took up residence in Council Hill and started calling himself Harvey Stump. The question is, why on Earth did Johnson go to Okmulgee, and who did he see while he was there?"

Holly's cheeks reddened as she listened to Scott ruminate aloud. If what he was saying was true, then Dan had lied to her yet again. She had begged Gee Dub not to tell anyone about their trip to Council Hill, but it was apparent to her now that once again she had behaved foolishly. "Sheriff Tucker," she said, "can I talk to you in private?"

Chapter Nineteen

Charles Tucker was used to taking charge of any situation, and it took some argument for Lavinia and Alafair to convince him it would be best to let them pursue their investigation quietly. Charles was a well-known figure around town and for him to show up at a stranger's funeral would be an occasion for comment. He was too intrigued to allow himself to be completely left out, though. So the three of them devised a plan whereby Charles would drive Lavinia and Alafair to the church at the corner of Seminole and Seventh and remain outside during the funeral. Then, if all went as expected, he would chauffeur the women to the cemetery, where they could all observe the burial from a distance. As for the post-burial reception, the most unobtrusive thing they could come up with was to park at the end of the street from the Johnson house and watch the "mourners" come and go.

Alafair and Lavinia waited until the service had begun before they slipped into the church and took a seat in a back pew. The plain pine coffin was situated at the front, under the pulpit. Alafair could only see the tip of a nose peeking up over the edge. She counted twenty people in the pews. Alafair expected it was only kinfolks who had come, and close family friends who could not otherwise get out of it. After the war and the massive death toll of the flu epidemic the previous year, everyone was funeraled out. From where she was sitting, Alafair could only see the backs of the family's heads. She leaned close to whisper in Lavinia's ear. "I can't tell anything about Johnson's folks from here."

"We'll get a look at them when we file by the coffin at the end of the service," Lavinia whispered back.

The preacher took the opportunity to try and convert any non-believers in the audience. He did not have much to say about the deceased. After the sermon Alafair and Lavinia followed the tiny congregation up the aisle to view the body and express sympathy to the bereaved.

The two women were last in line. Alafair took a long moment to observe the earthly remains of Daniel Johnson, who had caused such grief both in his life and in his death. The embalmers had only done a fair to middling job. The corpse had on too much makeup and the dark hair was parted in the middle and shiny with oil. His face looked a little lopsided. He did resemble the man in the photograph that Holly had shown her.

Alafair turned from the coffin to offer a hand and comforting words to the family. And finally get a good look at them.

Six people were sitting in the first row; two older couples, a young woman, and slightly removed, a younger man. The only people who looked like they had shed a tear was one of the older couples. Alafair pegged them as Dan's parents. The mother, if that's who she was, seemed to be nearly collapsed with grief. Her color was terrible, almost gray, and she was skeletally thin. The father looked distracted, as though he'd rather be anywhere but here. The other older couple were the widow's parents, judging by their solicitous manner toward the young woman. The girl's mother only had eyes for her daughter, but the man's face was like a thundercloud, dark and angry. The young woman, Dan's legal widow, Alafair expected, was a thin, fair-haired creature, almost fairy-like. Her black dress emphasized her white skin. She seemed confused, for which Alafair could not blame her. Discovering that your husband was alive when you thought he was dead, and then dead so soon after you find out he had been alive all along, would confuse and dismay anyone. As for the young man at the end of the pew, Alafair could not guess. A brother? The fiancé?

Alafair leaned down to offer a hand to the widow, who took it. The young woman's hands were cool and dry. She accepted Alafair's condolences with a somber, slightly curious expression that said, *Who are you, now?* Alafair responded with a smile, as though it was perfectly natural that she be there.

She and Lavinia circled back to their seats at the rear of the sanctuary. The preacher announced that there would be a gathering after the burial at the home of the dearly departed's parents, then the family filed down the aisle and out of the church.

Lavinia waited until the sanctuary was empty before she stood up. "Charles is outside, waiting to drive us out to the cemetery. We'd better get a move on if we aim to follow the funeral procession and see what we can see."

Chapter Twenty

Holly settled into the chair across the desk from Scott Tucker. The constable was gazing at her with an odd expression in his blue eyes. Curiosity? Suspicion? "I didn't want to tell you what happened the day Dan was killed, Sheriff Tucker, for fear you'll think my story makes me or Gee Dub look guilty. But we aren't. I did go to Council Hill. I hitched a ride on a truck with a delivery man. He dropped me off in front of the general store that is also the post office and the postmaster directed me to Harvey Stump's house. It wasn't but a couple of blocks away but it took me a little while to limp over there. I knocked on the front door and there was no answer for a long time, so I peeked in the window and saw a man lying on a chaise. He was smoking a cigarette. He had to have heard me knocking." She swallowed and her gaze flitted away. "He lifted up his head and looked at me. It was Dan.

"I went down there because I thought I had to know why he shamed me. But when I saw it really was him, all I wanted to do was get out of there. He recognized me right away and came tearing out the front door before I could get away. He grabbed my arm and clapped a hand over my mouth. I was scared, Sheriff. I was afraid he was going to hurt me, that he was going to panic because he had been found, and kill me or something. But that's not what happened at all. He took me inside and calmed me down, and we talked for almost an hour.

"He told me that he was sorry for the way he treated me. He said that he didn't mean to kill that man in Baltimore. They were fighting and the man fell and hit his head on the bar's marble countertop. Dan got scared and deserted. He planned to go up to Canada and disappear. He told me that he rode the rails at night to avoid the military police. He was panhandling outside the train station in Harrisburg when Harvey Stump offered to buy him a meal, and they got to talking. Harvey mentioned that he was from Council Hill, so close to Okmulgee, and that both his parents had died in the flu epidemic and had left Harvey quite a bit of money. So Dan saw an opportunity. He told Harvey that his name was Will Callahan. He said that his mother was real sick and if Harvey could see his way clear to loan him the price of a train ticket to Okmulgee, maybe he could make it home to see her one last time before she passed. Harvey said he'd be glad to do it. Dan told me he'd never known anybody like Harvey, that he was a truly good man, and he'd never met a truly good man before."

Holly hesitated. As she said it aloud, she heard for the first time what Dan's tale must sound like to someone who wasn't there.

Scott prompted her to continue. "But that's not the way it happened, is it?"

Holly's gaze drifted away. "No. Dan said that by the time they had to change trains in Muskogee, Harvey wasn't feeling so well and with the flu scare still going on the stationmaster wouldn't let him board. Dan didn't leave him, though. He had already had the flu while he was overseas. They found a farmer hauling hay to his place near Boynton and paid him to let them ride in the wagon bed. The plan was that when the farmer dropped them off at the crossroads outside Boynton, Dan could walk the last half-mile into town and rent a buggy for the rest of the trip to Council Hill. Dan told me that by the time he got back to where he left him, Harvey had died. He said he lost his nerve after that. He stole Harvey's ID, went to Council Hill and became Harvey Stump. Everybody in town just accepted that he was who he said he was, so he resolved to put his old life behind him and start anew."

Holly took a breath, wondering how much more she needed to say. *I'm a weak man,* Dan had told her. *All my life I been nothing but a disappointment to my parents and to anyone who ever loved me.*

"Did you ever love me?" he had asked her, and she had not been able to answer. "Dan Johnson is dead," he said to her then. "What good would it do to bring him back to life? My parents are used to me being gone. Pearl has moved on with her life and so should you. Believe me, you're both better off without me."

Scott Tucker had been jotting the occasional note on a piece of foolscap while she was talking. He did not look up. He did not tell her that he was inclined to believe Dan was more interested in getting his hands on Harvey's inheritance and escaping to nice warm Mexico than in starting anew, or even seeing his sick mother again. "Did you tell him that he had been found out and a U.S. marshal would be paying him a visit directly?"

"No. He didn't ask me how I found him and I didn't say. I told him that I was glad he had seen the light. He offered me money."

"Did you take it?"

She colored, but looked him in the eye. "I did. I suppose it really wasn't his to give, was it?"

"No."

"Do you think I'll have to give it back? It isn't enough to make up for what he did, but it's enough to get me back to Maine."

"I expect Harvey won't mind if you keep it," Scott said, his tone ironic. "Now, where does Gee Dub show up in this story?"

"After I left Dan, I went downtown to a cafe on Main Street. Gee Dub came in about ten or fifteen minutes later."

"How did he know where to find you?"

"He said it wasn't hard to figure out. Maybe after he got to Council Hill he saw me through the cafe window."

"Did he go to Johnson's house?"

Holly bit her lip. She had to tread carefully here. "I don't see how. I didn't see him while I was at Dan's. After Gee Dub came into the cafe, we were together from then until he gave me a ride back to his parents' farm."

Scott's expression did not betray his opinion of Holly's story. When she fell silent, he put the pencil down and clasped his hands together on the desktop. He studied her face for a moment before he spoke. "Miz Thornberry, what time of day did you get to Council Hill and when did you leave? According to Gee Dub's folks, you lit out from their farm in the middle of the day and didn't get back until nearly dawn the next morning. It's only six miles from Boynton to Council Hill. That's not the best road, but on a good day most folks can ride that far in less than an hour, either on horseback or in an auto. If you'd left Council Hill directly after your little adventure, you should have been back to the farm by suppertime. What were y'all doing all that time?"

She looked away again. "We didn't leave Council Hill right away. We sat in the cafe for a long time and ate and talked about what to do. There's only one place to eat there. You can ask them. They'll remember."

Scott was writing again. "This delivery man that you hitched a ride with, what was his name?"

"He told me to call him Royce. He said he was hauling a load of screws and bolts from Muskogee to Henryetta."

"Was there a sign on the side of the truck?"

"There was a name painted on the door. It said Ace Supply, Muskogee."

"It should be easy enough to check your story, Miz Thornberry. What time of day was it when this Royce picked you up?"

"I'm not sure. Mid-afternoon? Gee Dub's family was at the dinner table when I left the house and began walking toward the road. It must have taken me close to an hour to reach the main road. It felt like it, anyway. I don't walk very fast these days. I sat down on a big rock not far from the junction of the two roads. It didn't seem like I was there too long before the young man in the truck came by. He drove pretty fast most of the way, but there were parts of the road that were very bad. I could have walked the last few miles into Council Hill faster than Royce was able to drive. After I spoke to the man at the general store and post office, it took me maybe fifteen minutes to walk to the house where I found Dan."

While Holly was relating her tale, Scott was calculating. "Most folks generally have dinner around one, so if I figure right this meeting with Johnson ended around four, four-thirty. That fits in with when the neighbor lady heard a set-to over to Stump's house. So after you leave Johnson's house and go to the cafe, Gee Dub arrives and buys you dinner at the local eatery. Now, why didn't y'all ride straight to the law with the news that Stump was really Johnson? You must have known that after he saw you, he was going to leg it out of town as fast as he could go. Or did y'all know that Johnson wasn't going anywhere ever again?"

She stiffened and blurted, "Do you think I wanted anybody to know I'm even more of a fool than I look?" She clapped a hand over her mouth. "I'm sorry, Sheriff. I swear Dan was alive when I left his house. I begged Gee Dub not to tell anyone what I'd done. I must have looked a mess, sitting in that restaurant and sobbing like a baby. He was so kind I could hardly stand it."

"So you sat in the eatery all night long? That was mighty generous of the proprietor to let y'all sit there till dawn."

Holly's heart picked up speed. She could tell by the look on Scott Tucker's face that he was not buying it. She couldn't blame him. "If I tell you, will you promise not to spread it about?"

"Well, now, honey, you know I can't do that." Scott had already spoken the words when it dawned on him what she was probably going to say. He leaned back in his chair and crossed his arms. "I'll tell you what, Miz Thornberry. Depending on what you say to me, I'll try to tell as few folks as possible, if I can manage it. Believe me, darlin', you won't shock me. There is nothing new under the sun. But if you can give me something to help clear Gee Dub, you must do it."

Her face was red with embarrassment, now. "I think perhaps you have already figured it out, sir. After I left Dan, I went into the cafe to ask about the next train north. The waitress was alarmed at my state, so I told her a friend had died. She said

I should sit for a bit and pull myself together. Gee Dub came in. We drank some tea. We ate something. Afterwards we rode double to Boynton. Back to the farm. Back to his room. It was after dark when we got in. He said I should clean up before I went back to the house. But…the next thing I knew, it was nearly dawn."

She was relieved that Scott did not look scandalized. He nodded. "That explains where you two were all night and that's helpful. Still, we don't know when Gee Dub got to Council Hill. Maybe he followed you and was lurking about outside Stump's house the whole time you were there. Did Gee Dub tell you where he was between the time you left Johnson and before he came into the cafe?"

"He did not."

Something about the way her eyes skittered when she said it gave Scott pause. "He didn't?"

"No, he didn't tell me anything." Her firm tone let him know that she was not going to say any more than that.

Chapter Twenty-one

Phoebe Day was on a mission. The Tucker siblings had divvied up their investigative tasks and her assignment was to go through Gee Dub's room, ostensibly to pack a few things for his comfort into the empty gunny sack she was carrying. A change of shirt, some extra drawers and undershirts, socks. Phoebe's real task was to look for anything in that room that could be used in Gee Dub's defense.

Phoebe's husband, John Lee Day, was in charge of both the Tucker farm and the Day farm this week, since Shaw was meeting with Abner Meriwether in Muskogee and Alafair had gone to Okmulgee to attend Dan Johnson's funeral. Sophronia and Grace were desolate at being excluded from ransacking Gee Dub's room, but Alafair and Shaw had let Blanche stay home from school to help Phoebe. It would not have done if all three of the Tucker schoolchildren had played hooky. Mary Lucas was watching Phoebe's three little children while her sisters conducted their search.

As Phoebe walked from the back door of her parents' house to the bunk room behind the barn, she set such a pace that her assistant searcher Blanche had trouble keeping up with her. Even their volunteer companion Charlie Dog had to break into a trot in order not to be left behind. Blanche squeaked with alarm when the hunting party was strafed by the mother mockingbird, but Phoebe was too intent on the task at hand to spare more than an impatient wave at the bird as she opened the door to the toolshed and marched back to the bunk room.

Blanche began her search by looking under the pillows on both cots. She had already heard about the cartridge boxes, both empty now. She placed them carefully on the crate that Gee Dub had been using for a bedside table before stripping back the covers. "Phoebe, why do you suppose Mama made up both beds, if only Gee is staying here for now?"

Phoebe didn't look up from rifling through the drawers in the chest by the back wall. "I don't know. She probably thought it looks better, more lived-in, don't you know." She removed a couple of neatly folded long-sleeved shirts and laid them atop the chest. She paused when she saw a velvet-covered box pushed back into the corner of the drawer. She opened it to find three pendants suspended from colored ribbons; a cross with eagle on it, a star, and a purple heart with a cameo of George Washington in the middle.

She sat down heavily on the end of one of the cots with the box in her lap.

"What did you find?" Blanche said.

"Medals. Blanche, did Gee Dub ever say anything about being wounded while he was overseas?"

"Wounded? No, not that I ever heard. He doesn't have any scars that I can see, nor is he missing any limbs. Why do you think he was wounded?"

"See this?" She held up the purple heart. "A soldier only gets this if he's wounded in combat."

"Well, he never said."

Phoebe put the medal back into the box with the others. "No, he wouldn't. He never was much of a 'sayer'."

Blanche sat down next to her. "What are those other ones?"

"I don't know what they are for. But it looks like our brother may be some kind of war hero. That's good! We'll give these to Mr. Meriwether. Nobody is going to want to put a war hero in jail." She stood and placed the medals on top of the pile of clothing. "I'm going to pack up these clothes and the rest. You look in that bottom drawer and see if you can find anything else that might be useful."

Blanche was eager to comply, and for a few moments there was silence as the sisters concentrated on their tasks. Half of the bottom drawer contained half-a-dozen jars of preserved fruits and vegetables that Gee Dub must have liberated from Alafair's pantry. "Why do you suppose Gee has a stash of food from Mama's pantry? Looks like he's been eating watermelon rind preserves directly out of the jar."

"Watermelon rind preserves was always one of his favorites," Phoebe answered absently.

"Why keep a cache, when he could just eat as much as he wants up to the house?" Blanche didn't wait for an answer. She held up a packet of letters. "Lookie here, Phoebe. Do you think we ought to read them?"

Phoebe's brow knit. She took the letters from Blanche and shuffled through them. "I hate to. These are Gee Dub's private letters. I see several from Mama, and from the rest of us, too. Here are some that look official, from the Army and all. We ought to give these to Mr. Meriwether, as well as the medals. He can ask Gee about them. Maybe there is something in one of these letters that he can use."

"Here's a pair of backpacks under this blanket," Blanche said.

Phoebe began stuffing clothing and the found items into the gunny sack. "What's in them?"

"This one is empty. It has 'Tucker, Lt. George W' stenciled on the flap. This other one…It's got one of them Army caps in it. Leggings. Couple other things of the like. Here's a canteen."

There was a pause, and Phoebe looked up from her folding. "What is it?"

Blanche was gazing at the name on the flap. "Phoebe, who is Private R.J. Moretti?"

Chapter Twenty-two

Alafair and Lavinia mingled with the crowd outside the First Methodist Episcopal Church until the pallbearers came out with the casket containing the earthly remains of Daniel Johnson and slid it into the hearse. They stood discreetly in a corner beside the church door until all the mourners had gotten into their conveyances—a horse-drawn buggy, a couple of automobiles, and two men riding horseback. The widow and her parents briskly departed the church, but the deceased's mother could hardly keep her feet. The father practically had to carry her down the steps and lift her into the brougham following the hearse. The young man who had sat with the family at the funeral gave Alafair and Lavinia a narrow look as he rode by on a blaze-faced quarter horse and fell into line behind the last auto. As the procession pulled out of the dirt lot next to the church, the young fellow turned in the saddle to shoot one last curious glance at the strangers. Once the cortege rounded the corner, Alafair and Lavinia walked over to Charles, who was still sitting in his town car parked across the street from the church, trying to look inconspicuous. They climbed into the backseat and Charles pulled out to follow the procession at a distance.

The internment was already underway by the time Charles parked behind some cedars at the top of a knoll overlooking the graveyard, an unobtrusive spot from which to watch the proceedings. There were fewer people at the burial than had attended the funeral. Alafair had a perfect view of the family gathered around the open grave.

The three Tuckers stood for a long moment, observing.

Charles finally broke the silence. "I know that man holding the widow's arm. That's Bertram Evans. Suppose he's her father? He's a local builder and a good customer. Buys a lot of finished board from the sawmill. He's well-off, to say the least. I reckon any man would consider his daughter a good catch."

"That widow is one pretty gal," Lavinia noted.

Alafair nodded. The widow was very pretty indeed. She was clinging to her father's arm, and making a point of leaning for support on any man who offered his condolences. Perhaps shedding a tear on his sleeve. *She's just the kind of woman certain men like, all weak and helpless.* Alafair scolded herself for the uncharitable thought. After all, she didn't know the slightest thing about the woman.

"Charles," she said, "do you know that young fellow there who has been hovering around the widow since the funeral? He was sitting in the family pew."

Charles squinted at the dark-haired man with his hands in his pockets who was standing slightly behind young Mrs. Johnson. "I can't see him too well from here, but I don't recognize him right off."

Lavinia shaded her eyes with her hand for a better view. "He is friends with the widow's daddy, for sure. Look how he leans in to talk with him. Maybe he works for her daddy and is looking to get on his good side by cosseting the daughter. Or maybe he's her brother or some other kin."

Alafair shook her head. "That was my first thought, too, until I got a good look at him at the church. He's no brother, unless her folks found him under a cabbage leaf. He don't favor that family one whit. Last week, when Scott came over here with Miz Thornberry to talk to Dan's parents, Johnson Senior told him that the widow was aiming to remarry. I'll bet money that is the prospective groom."

Lavinia eagerly latched on to this information. "Remarry! Alafair, that's a motive for murder right there. The young gal figures she's moving on with her life, got her a fine new fellow who never killed anybody or deserted the Army or married an extra wife, and what does she find out but that she's still shackled to the man who left her high and dry."

Charles agreed with his wife's assessment. "And what about her betrothed, if that's who he is? Here he's found himself a beautiful, wealthy woman to marry and before he can say 'I do', her late husband pops up from the grave."

"I think that is Dan's mother, the one who can hardly stand on her own." Alafair pointed her out. "Either her son's passing has like to killed her or she's ailing something awful."

"Well, this speculation is fine and good, but I reckon we'd find out a lot more if we could actually ask them," Lavinia said.

"I sure would like a chance to have a word with some of those folks," Alafair admitted. "We ought to go to the reception."

Charles snorted. "What could you say to the family aside from 'I'm sorry for your loss'?"

Alafair pondered a moment before she turned and gave Lavinia a conspiratorial look. "What say you and me invite ourselves over to express our condolences to the family this evening, after the reception is done with and everybody has left? Here's what we'll say—we're both mothers of war veterans. That's no lie. We'll tell them that we've been attending as many funerals of veterans as we can so as to show support to the families."

"And that is a lie," Lavinia said.

"Well, it is true that I haven't heard of any other veteran funerals over the past year, so none is as many as I could have attended. How about you?"

"Just the son of one of Charles' customers, but he was buried in France and they only had a memorial for him at the Catholic Church."

"Did you go?"

"We did. Neither of us had ever been inside a Catholic Church before."

"Well, then, there you go. It's no lie that we have attended as many veterans' memorials as we were able."

"If you present yourselves at the reception, I'm coming with you," Charles informed them. "Y'all girls don't need to be going into the lion's den on your own."

Perhaps Charles really was concerned for their safety, but Alafair suspected that he simply didn't want to be left out again. "Come along, then. If you are acquainted with Mr. Evans, maybe he'll take a notion to tell you something about his late son-in-law that will help our case."

Chapter Twenty-three

Abner Meriwether, Attorney at Law, settled himself across the table from his client. "I've been doing some research on you, Gee Dub."

Gee Dub was surprised to hear that. "Have you, now? You've known me since I was knee high."

Meriwether pulled a sheaf of papers from his briefcase and spread them out in front of himself. "You've done a few things over the past year and a half that your family doesn't know about. Your sister Phoebe found something she didn't expect while she was packing up a change of clothes for you. Seems the U.S. Army has a high opinion of you. So much so that they gave you some hardware before they let you go." Meriwether paused in case Gee Dub had a comment about this, but none was forthcoming so he went on. "The one that interested me the most was the Purple Heart."

Gee Dub's mouth quirked. "You don't have to do anything to get one of those. Just sit still and let a mortar fall on you."

"I contacted the Army Records Office. Apparently you had a pretty bad knock on the head. Says here you were out cold for two days."

"So they tell me."

"Woke up in the field hospital and got sent back to the front a week later. Attached to a British unit. That seems like a mighty quick turn-around time for somebody who just had his head cracked. Tell me, have you had any lasting effects from the incident?"

Gee Dub could see where this was going. He sat back in the chair and studied his lawyer from under his eyelashes. "Mr. Meriwether, do you have a point?"

For a few seconds, Meriwether absently tapped his pen on the tabletop, considering. "Gee Dub, I am well aware that men who have lived through war, or worse, suffered grievous injuries, can be permanently changed by the experience. I am acquainted with a woman whose husband was gassed over in France, and this fine young man will never be the same. He can hardly remember his own name for two minutes at a time."

"So your defense is going to be that I'm not of sound mind?"

Meriwether smiled. "Obviously, no one who talked to you for ten minutes would believe that. But the lingering effects of trauma could very possibly allow a man to do things he would never have done before the injury."

"Mr. Meriwether, you ever been to war?"

"No, but..."

"Well, then, let me enlighten you. Soldiers get maimed and hurt and killed, sure. But at least soldiers can defend themselves. They give you a gun and send you into harm's way with a bunch of other guys with guns all around you. But it's the innocent who suffer the most. Women and little kids and old folks who don't want to hurt anybody. Their men get taken away from them, and then they get robbed and bombed and shot and brutalized and they're helpless..." He swallowed his words, suddenly aware that he was rambling. He took a breath and returned to the topic at hand.

"The doctor in charge of the field hospital thought I was in good enough shape to return to duty after a week, and I managed to do everything they asked of me after that. I don't think this is a productive line of inquiry."

"It's my job to pursue every line of inquiry, son. I want to make sure I leave no possible stone unturned."

"Well, leave off this particular stone, Mr. Meriwether. I don't want to end up in the insane asylum any more than I want to go to prison."

Meriwether studied his client's face for a long moment. Gee Dub had no intention of discussing the matter right now, but neither did Meriwether intend to forget about it. "Whatever you say. We'll talk more about a defense when and if you are indicted."

• • ● ● •

The Newcastle boys had been losing soldiers to a German sharp-shooter at a mighty clip. That was why Anderson had requested a sharpshooter of his own. Or at least somebody who could shoot straight. Not one of those English boys could hit the side of a barn with a handful of beans. Fritz—that's what they called the German who had been taking them out—spent his days waiting for somebody to poke an eye over the lip of the trench. The English boys were scared shitless. They acted like Fritz had a special power. Gee Dub shook his head at the memory. Anderson had to whip on them with that crop he carried around just to get them to do anything that required standing up straight.

Fritz wasn't such a much, though. Gee Dub tested him out as soon as he got there by sticking a hat on the end of a bayonet. Fritz was watching them. He knew that a lorry had dropped somebody off up the road. He probably figured that he had a bunch of green replacements to do target practice on. He fired twice at the hat. Rapid—bang, bang. The first bullet came from about thirty degrees to Gee Dub's left and took a chunk out of the brim. The second was a clean miss. Gee Dub had his number after that. He hauled the nearest Tommy out of his hole in the mud and set him up with the hat and the bayonet a couple of yards down the ditch. The young Englishman was shaking so hard that Gee Dub was afraid Fritz wouldn't be able to get a bead on the target, but the movement did make it look like the hat was on a head. Fritz fired and the Tommy dropped the bayonet in a panic, but that split second was all Gee Dub needed. Fritz didn't have his pointy hat on, but in the one blink it took Gee Dub to aim, he could see that the German had gray in his brown hair and that his eyes were blue. Gee Dub got him clean. After that, he could have told those English boys that the sun rises in the west and they would have done their best to believe him.

"Tucker?"

Gee Dub started and looked at the guard standing beside him. Meriwether had gone.

"Time to go back to your cell," the guard said.

Chapter Twenty-four

Pearl Evans Johnson had been in hell for the past two weeks. The first time her feckless husband Dan Johnson died, that had been a shock, it was true. But she had moved on most satisfactorily. In fact, she had found someone to marry who was way better than Dan. She had married Dan Johnson in a haze, not more than a month before he was called up and left for basic training. He had been charming and his parents were well-respected, and the fact that he might be going to his doom was so romantic. The wedding night was a revelation to her, and their newlywed bliss was quite enough to carry her through to his departure. But he was gone for such a long time, and she was young and pretty and the boys hovered around like bees. She was good, though, and stayed faithful to her soldier for as long as any human person could reasonably expect.

Until her father's assistant, Leon Stryker, declared his affection. Loving Leon was torment, for what could she do about it? No woman in her right mind would voluntarily get a divorce, especially not from a soldier who was overseas fighting for his country. Then the war ended, and Dan's letters ended, and the next thing she knew he had killed a man in a fight, gone AWOL, and died of the flu by the side of the road outside of Boynton.

Then one day out of the blue some lawman from Boynton had come to Pearl's little bungalow and told her that Dan was probably still alive. In which case her much-anticipated wedding to her beloved, kind, so handsome Leon Stryker could not be.

She was devastated. Until a couple of days later she found out that her resurrected husband got himself shot through the heart and her problem was solved.

She felt bad that his latest and final death made her so happy, but not so bad that she didn't immediately reinstate her wedding plans. Dan's parents had been good to her, especially his father, so after Dan's second demise she was careful to maintain the proper deportment for a young war widow. In fact, she rather enjoyed the sympathy she was receiving and didn't see any difficulty about milking it while she could. Besides, come the fall, after all the folderol had died down, she'd get to be a bride again.

After they returned from the cemetery, she had sat for hours in the middle of her mother-in-law's parlor and received mourners with the gracious good manners expected of a lady. Dan's mother and father were on the settee next to her armchair, broken with grief. Pearl's own mother had stepped in to act as hostess. Her father did his duty as greeter. Pearl appreciated the fact that he was there at all. He had only come to the funeral because Pearl had begged him. Bertram Evans had had a low opinion of Dan when he was alive, and that opinion had not improved now that Dan was dead.

Leon kept a respectable distance from Pearl throughout the day, but his presence gave her the strength to get through this ordeal. He had made sure that he was always in her line of sight, ready to exchange a loving glance when no one was watching. The crowd began to thin out at the same time as the buffet table, and Pearl was considering whether or not she had finally done her duty well enough to go home and have some time alone with Leon. No new guests had shown up for a while, and the two or three who were still there were standing at the sideboard, polishing off the last of the spread.

Pearl was tucking her handkerchief into her sleeve and preparing to depart when the two women and the distinguished man came in.

Pearl leaned toward her mother-in-law and murmured,

"Mother Johnson, those people yonder were at the funeral. Do you know who they are?"

Mrs. Johnson rallied herself enough to look up, but she didn't get the chance to reply before the women came over to pay their respects.

• ● ● ● ●

The Tuckers had already formulated a plan of action. As soon as they entered the Johnson house, each made a beeline for her or his object of inquiry. Charles headed for Bertram Evans, his business associate and the widow's father, who was standing next to the wall beside Leon Stryker. Lavinia's assignment was to see what she could learn from the widow.

Alafair had claimed the parents of the deceased for herself. She knew she was taking advantage of their grief and distraction, but she didn't care. Honesty would not bring Dan Johnson back from the dead, nor would consideration for their feelings save Gee Dub from a murder charge.

Mrs. Johnson's sunken eyes were bleary with tears and her expression was vague, but Fern Johnson, Dan's father, gave Alafair a curious once-over as she knelt down on the floor in front of the settee. She took the mother's hand in both of her own. "Miz Johnson, my name is Miz Shaw Tucker. I'm sister-in-law to Charles and Lavinia Tucker. That's them yonder. Lavinia and me are founders of the Society for Mothers of Veterans, Okmulgee Chapter. Both of us are the mothers of wounded soldiers. It is our solemn privilege to offer whatever support we can to the families of war casualties. We know your boy was a veteran, and we want to let you know that if there is anything we can do for you, you only need to ask."

Alafair was not sure that Mrs. Johnson was paying attention, or even aware of her surroundings, until she said, "I saw y'all at the funeral. You were at the cemetery, too."

So much for discreet observation, Alafair thought. "Yes, ma'am. We try to attend the funerals of as many veterans as we can and show support to the families."

Fern Johnson's eyes widened. "Tucker of Tucker Lumber Company? Is that y'all? Did you know Dan?"

"Yes, sir, my brother-in-law Charles owns the Tucker Lumber Company. No, I'm sorry to say that I never knew your late son. But I know he served his country. Was he in Europe?"

"Yes, he was in England," Mrs. Johnson said. "But he did not die in the war, you know."

Mr. Johnson put a hand on his wife's arm. "Mother…"

"That doesn't matter, ma'am," Alafair assured her. "He was still a veteran. How did he meet his end at such a young age?"

Mrs. Johnson's expression sharpened and she appeared to see Alafair for the first time. "Why, someone killed him. You didn't know that? That is all anyone in town has been able to talk about since it happened."

Fern Johnson flopped back in his seat with a sigh. It was futile to try and manage a mother's emotions on this day of her child's funeral.

Alafair dropped the woman's hand, feigning shock. She spoke quickly before Mr. Johnson could try again to restore his wife's sense of discretion. "Oh, my goodness. I'm so sorry. Okmulgee is a big town and I had not heard the particulars. What happened?"

"A robbery? I don't know. Someone shot him dead in his own garage."

Alafair swallowed. "Do they know who did it?"

"The police told us that they'd keep us informed, but we haven't heard anything."

They would soon. Still, Alafair was relieved that the Johnsons had not heard Gee Dub's name yet. If they had already been told that a Tucker had been arrested on suspicion of killing their son, there would be no chance they'd tell her anything.

Alafair was beginning to feel impatient. She wanted an answer to her real question. Why was it that Dan's parents hadn't cared what happened to their son the first time he died, but were prostrate with grief over his second death?

Perhaps her desperate desire to know had caused the question to manifest in the ether, because Mrs. Johnson said, "Our poor Dan had been given a second chance. He was turning his life around."

Mr. Johnson paled and leaned forward to put himself between Alafair and his wife. Alafair drew back, startled. Mrs. Johnson seemed equally surprised by her husband's move, especially when he put a hand on her shoulder and shoved her back into her seat. "Thank you for coming, Miz Tucker," he said. "It's good to know that there are some folks in town who care about our soldier boys."

• • ● ● •

"I'll tell you, Bertram Evans was not in the least broke up about his son-in-law's death," Charles said. Alafair and her in-laws had driven directly back to Charles and Lavinia's house from the reception, and were exchanging information around the mahogany table in the dining room with coffee and cookies. "He was eager to tell me and anybody else who'd listen that Dan was a fugitive who stole another man's life. He wasn't a bit shy with his opinion that Dan was a ne'er-do-well and his daughter Pearl was well shet of him. And you were right about the young fellow being the widow's beau, Alafair. His name is Leon Stryker. He's the accountant and financial officer for Evans' business, and I suppose you could say he's Evans' apprentice, too. The two of them look to be thick as thieves."

"If that's the case, I reckon Mr. Evans is not unhappy that his daughter is finally free to marry Leon," Alafair said.

Lavinia nodded. "And wouldn't Leon be overjoyed to become part of his boss' family? So Leon must have been dismayed when he learned that his betrothed's first husband was not dead after all."

Charles lifted his shoulders. "Evans told me that Pearl is his only child, so if Leon was to marry her he would eventually inherit the construction company. To be fair, though, Leon does seem to be besotted with Pearl, so it's probably a love match, as well as a handy business arrangement."

He paused long enough to reach for another cookie. "I made so bold as to ask Evans how they took it when they first heard that Dan might be alive. Leon acted like he was most concerned about Pearl's feelings. He said that Dan's resurrection would have delayed their wedding in a big way. But Pearl had plenty of grounds for divorce and he was willing to wait until she was free. Evans couldn't even stand to hear Dan Johnson's name. His face got so red that I feared his head was going to blow off. He really hated the son-of-a-gun. If some yahoo had treated my daughter that way, I would hate him, too."

"I didn't get anything useful out of the widow," Lavinia admitted. "I couldn't figure out a way to bring up the circumstances of her late husband's second death. It didn't seem right to say, 'congratulations on your narrow escape.' I did commiserate with her on her loss, and she smiled that little cat smile of hers and said that she had reconciled herself to what had happened."

"I think the parents knew Dan was still alive," Alafair said. "I think they were in contact with him, too. Maybe the whole time he was in Council Hill."

Lavinia straightened in her chair, surprised. "Goodness. Alafair, what makes you say that?"

"The mother told me that Dan had been given a second chance and was turning his life around. How would she know that if she had just found out where he had been? Besides, when she said that, the father like to knocked her off the settee in order to shut her up."

Lavinia clapped a hand to her chest. "If they knew Dan was alive all along, that would explain why they weren't interested in claiming poor Harvey Stump's body."

"Wouldn't it, though?"

"Let's think about this, then." Charles uncapped his fancy Parker fountain pen and began making a list on the back of an envelope. "Who had a reason to want Dan Johnson to stay dead? Pearl had the best motive, but she seems an unlikely killer. Gently brought-up young women don't usually go around shooting people in the heart from a foot away."

Lavinia tapped the table with her index finger. "Gently brought-up young ladies can pull a trigger as well as anybody, Charles. But I vote for Leon as the probable murderer. If Pearl came crying to him that Dan was alive and a bigamist, to boot, he could have been overcome with chivalrous intent. He could easily have ridden that blaze-faced horse of his to Council Hill that very evening and avenged his beloved's honor."

"Pearl's daddy had just as much reason to worry about the family honor as Leon did," Charles noted.

Alafair sighed. "I hate to do it, but you ought to put Holly on that suspect list, too, Charles. Nobody was more wronged by that wastrel than Holly. She traveled halfway across America to find him, just to discover that he had played her for a fool and taken everything from her, even her good name. I wouldn't blame her a bit if it was her who shot him."

The three of them fell silent for a moment. Neither Charles nor Lavinia had the heart to point out to Alafair that they had left one very possible suspect off the list.

Charles laid his pen on the table. "We know the date that Scott came down here and told the Johnsons that the body Clelland Rogers found in December is not their son. If Alafair is right, and his parents already knew that Dan was alive and living in Council Hill, why didn't they rush over there that very day and tell him that he was about to be found out? Why would he hang around after that and wait to be discovered?"

"If Dan had already told his folks that he took Harvey Stump's identity," Alafair said, "they might have been confident that nobody would be able to figure out who the dead man was or where he came from. Harvey is long-buried, after all, and nobody has ever come looking for him. Dan's parents wouldn't know that Scott had Harvey's identification disc."

Lavinia shook her head, perplexed. "Well, whoever killed Dan had just found out where he was. Somebody spilled the beans to the wrong person."

"We know which of the people at the funeral might have wanted Dan Johnson dead." Alafair reached across the table and picked up Charles' list. "Now we have to find out where each of them was on the night that Dan was killed."

Chapter Twenty-five

Alafair forced herself to wait until the sun was up before making her way from Lavinia's house to Pearl Johnson's bungalow. Lavinia had offered to come with her, but Alafair planned to leave for Boynton straight from Pearl's house. She had telephoned Shaw at his aunt's house in Muskogee the night before and learned that Gee Dub had been granted bail and was due to be released this morning, but could not leave Muskogee before the hearing. Shaw and Alafair had kept the long-distance telephone call short so as not to bankrupt Charles, but they had been able to exchange a lot of information in three minutes. Meriwether had convinced the judge that Gee Dub was not a flight risk, Shaw told her. It was also helpful that the judge had a soft spot for newly returned veterans. Besides, Shaw had put up the farm for collateral. Yesterday evening Alice and Holly had driven Walter Kelley's Model T all the way to Muskogee, bursting to tell Lawyer Meriwether what they had learned from S.B. Turner at the livery stable—sometime before he took over Harvey Stump's house and life in Council Hill, Dan Johnson rented a horse in Boynton and rode to Okmulgee.

Shaw, Gee Dub, and Meriwether had scheduled a planning session at the lawyer's Muskogee office that evening, after Gee Dub's release. Shaw was feeling hopeful. Gee Dub was oddly calm about the whole situation.

Alafair couldn't say the same about herself. There was so much more to find out about Dan Johnson's death, and so little time to uncover it.

The widow Pearl Johnson's bungalow was set back from the street, almost hidden from view by shrubbery and overhanging trees. The frame siding was painted light green, which made a pleasant backdrop for the newly budded spirea and forsythia bushes planted all along the front of the house. It was a little too early for blossoms on the two bare redbuds at the side of the walk, but in a month or so, the front door of Pearl Johnson's little house would be framed by lavender blooms.

Alafair parked the buggy in the street and climbed down. She took a minute to treat her long-suffering mare to a nose-bag of oats while she thought about how she was going to go about this. She had no idea how Pearl Johnson would receive her, especially at this early hour, but she determined that, if she had to, she would stand outside and pound on the door until Pearl agreed to talk to her.

It wasn't necessary for Alafair to storm the enemy's citadel. It only took a minute or two for Pearl to answer Alafair's knock. The young woman was clad in a pale green dressing gown, her blond tresses unbound and hanging down her back and over her shoulders in charming disarray. The aroma wafting from the coffee mug in Pearl's hand reminded Alafair that she had left Lavinia's in too much of a rush for breakfast.

Pearl did not seem taken aback to see who was at her door. "Good morning, Miz Tucker. You're out and about early. What can I do for you?"

Alafair blinked. Pearl looked different this morning. Not nearly so helpless. Older, perhaps. "I'm surprised you remember me, Miz Johnson, what with so many well-wishers coming and going at your in-laws' house yesterday."

"Of course I remember you, Miz Tucker, and your sister-in-law, Miz Charles Tucker. You said you were representing the... what was it? The Society of Mothers of Veterans? Y'all were very kind. I was surprised and gratified that you could find the time to attend to your Society duties yesterday, especially after Chief Bowman came by here late last evening to tell me that one George W. Tucker has been arrested on suspicion of having murdered Dan. I'm guessing that fact must be of interest to you."

Alafair felt like she had been kicked in the chest. She had been seriously mistaken when she pegged Pearl Johnson as a lightweight. Alafair regrouped quickly and decided that the direct approach was her best option. "George W. Tucker is my son, Miz Johnson. He was arrested earlier this week, but he has not been charged with anything. I'm sorry that I wasn't honest with you. As you can imagine, I do not believe for a minute that my son killed your husband, and I will do anything I can to prove him innocent. I'm sorry you lost your husband, but surely you want his real killer to be convicted of the crime and not just the person most convenient to hand."

Pearl lowered her head and for a moment gazed at Alafair thoughtfully, taking stock. Her careful expression made it hard to judge how she felt. Alafair sagged with relief when Pearl stood aside and invited her in with a gesture. The young widow led her through a small but well-appointed parlor, out the French doors at the back of the house and onto a shady, flower-lined brick patio. A round ironwork table beside the back door held a plate of warm biscuits, pots of jam and butter, and a silver coffeepot. Alafair's arrival had interrupted breakfast. Pearl removed an extra mug from a cabinet under the window and invited Alafair to sit.

Alafair was too anxious to observe the niceties. "Miz Johnson, I have to ask you…"

Pearl didn't let her finish. "Don't worry, Miz Tucker, I have no desire to see your son go to jail for shooting Dan." She filled the empty mug with coffee and set it in front of Alafair before resuming her seat. "Or anyone, for that matter. Whatever led to Dan's death, I'm sure he brought it on himself." The look on Alafair's face made her smile. "Have I shocked you?"

Alafair managed to smile back. "Considering what little I know about Dan, I suppose not."

"I'm not sure how you think I can help you, though. I have no idea who shot Dan or who had a particularly good reason to. I don't know what he had been up to. Like everybody else, I thought he died of the flu in December and was buried up in Boynton. I had no idea he was still alive until your Boynton sheriff told me so."

Alafair reached for a biscuit while she considered how to frame her questions. She scooped a spoonful of strawberry jam and dropped it onto her china saucer. Pearl did not press her, instead waiting patiently for her guest to say whatever she had come to say.

Alafair took a breath and began. "You know that Dan married another woman last year up in New England."

Pearl leaned her elbows on the table and clasped her hands under her chin. "I do now. Dan always did do whatever struck his fancy and never mind the consequences. Mother Johnson told me that the other woman came to the house with the sheriff. I wish I'd seen her. I'm curious to know what she had that Dan just couldn't do without."

"Her name is Holly Thornberry, and believe me, she is just as much a victim in all this as you are. She had no idea Dan was already married."

Pearl raised one eyebrow. "You've met her? How do you know her? What is she like?"

"My son, George…we call him Gee Dub…met up with Miz Thornberry a few days ago when she crossed a field on our farm and needed some help with directions. She's had a hard life, I think. A nice girl. Impulsive, though. She doesn't much think things through."

"Impulsive. They probably suited each other fine then." Pearl sounded amused.

"My family got involved in all this by accident, Miz Johnson. Gee Dub was not acquainted with Dan Johnson at all and had no reason to kill him. Miz Thornberry came to Oklahoma to find the man she thought was her husband because she wanted to know what had happened to him. She wanted to know why he had deserted her, or if he was even still alive."

Pearl had been listening to Alafair with an expression of mild interest. "I was well-acquainted with Dan's persuasive ability. I'm sure it happened just as Miz Thornberry said. After she and the Boynton sheriff came here to speak with Dan's parents, my father-in-law told me how she reacted when she found out that he was already married. I don't blame her for running away. I was just as shocked and humiliated when I found out about her."

"I heard that you have recently become engaged to your father's assistant, Leon Stryker."

Pearl's eyes softened. "That is true."

"It must have been distressing to both of you to hear that Dan could be alive."

If Pearl understood Alafair's implication, she didn't show it. "Indeed it was, Miz Tucker. I did not relish the idea of going through a divorce, even though no one who knows the situation would blame me. Still, divorce carries such a taint. After the way Dan behaved, I would have done it, though. Even if I'd never met Leon."

"Divorce takes a long time," Alafair pointed out.

"It does. I don't think that murdering Dan would be a reasonable shortcut, though." For the first time, Pearl's voice took on a sharp tone.

"Miz Johnson, I don't mean to imply…"

"Of course you do. But I didn't do it, I promise you that. It all happened so fast, finding out that Dan could be alive and then hearing that he had been killed. I didn't have time to formulate a plan. I could hardly believe it was happening. Now that I've had time to think about it, I'm furious at Dan, and furious at myself for falling for his balderdash in the first place. I'm relieved I don't have to deal with him anymore. I wish there were something I could say that would help you, but I really don't know who shot Dan."

"You know that if my son goes to trial someone from the defender's office will want to question you. They'll want to know where you were when Dan was shot."

Pearl's forehead wrinkled as she considered this. "When was Dan shot, exactly?"

Alafair hesitated. If she told her exactly when Dan died, would she be giving Pearl an opportunity to concoct an alibi? But she was curious to hear what Pearl would have to say. "Last anybody saw him alive that I know of was late on the afternoon of the twenty-seventh. I was told that Dan's neighbor heard a shot at about seven o'clock that night. But no one has decided for sure that was the shot that killed him."

Pearl sat back in her chair, figuring. "Was that Thursday before last? Yes, the twenty-seventh. That was the evening that I had supper with Leon at his sister's house. Yes, I'm sure. She had some other people over. There will be lots of witnesses." Her expression lightened.

She's relieved that Leon has an alibi, too, Alafair thought. Pearl was surely aware that no matter what he may have told her, her fiancé also had an excellent motive for murder. On the other hand, Alafair was trying to hide her disappointment that two of her most likely suspects could account for their whereabouts at seven o'clock on the evening of February 27th. If in fact that really was the hour of Dan Johnson's murder.

Alafair pushed her plate away, her appetite gone. "I do appreciate you taking the time to talk to me, Miz Johnson. I know this is a strange situation. Not many a widow would be willing to speak to the mother of the man suspected of killing her husband."

Pearl's guarded manner had disappeared. She was downright chipper. "Well, he wasn't much of a husband, Miz Tucker. To tell you the truth, I'm glad to be free of him. Dan wasn't a bad man, really. He was charming and funny. He had a knack for making you feel like you were the most interesting person who ever lived. He didn't mean to hurt folks. He just never wasted one moment's thought on anybody but himself. It didn't take me long to see my mistake, especially once I got to know Leon and saw what an honorable man really looks like. My father is thrilled at the match."

Alafair stood up. "I'm sorry to have bothered you."

"Oh, no bother at all. In fact I'm glad you came by." She stood as well. "I'll see you out."

"Miz Johnson, you said it was last night when the police chief told you about my son's arrest?"

"Yes, it was."

"Do you think Dan's parents have been told as well?"

"I know they have. After Chief Bowman left, I went across the street to tell them myself, but they already knew. The chief went there first. I reckon he thought Dan's mother would be more interested than I would."

"Do you think they would be willing to talk to me?"

The idea seemed to amuse Pearl. "I wouldn't try it, if I was you. When I went over there last night, Mother Johnson was already ranting about how the Tucker lawman from Boynton and the passel of Tuckers who came to the funeral had to be somehow connected to the Tucker who killed her baby. She's liable to throw you out on your ear." Pearl hooked an arm through one of Alafair's and escorted her to the front door as though they were the best of friends. "You know, Mother Johnson has to bear a lot of responsibility for the way Dan turned out. She just never would hear a bad word against him. Not like Father Johnson. Dan was always a big disappointment to him, and I think it was no surprise to him that Dan came to a bad end. It was him who didn't even want to claim Dan's body the first time we thought he was dead. I figured Mother Johnson would throw a hissy fit at that, but I guess she decided she wouldn't budge her husband, so why try? But when Dan died the second time, I suppose Father Johnson just didn't have the strength to deny her again. I'm sure you saw that Mother Johnson is not well. In fact, we've been told that she cannot live much longer. It would have been cruel of Father Johnson to let her leave this Earth without finally throwing a funeral for her darling Dan."

Alafair decided that if she didn't ask now, she'd never have a better chance. "Could it be that Dan's folks knew he was alive and living in Council Hill? Maybe that's why his mother didn't argue about a funeral the first time he died."

This was the first thing that Alafair had said since she arrived that seemed to surprise Pearl. "Oh, my, I never considered that. I don't know. Surely, they would have told me. If they knew Dan was alive, surely Mother Johnson would have said something when I told them of my plans to remarry. I don't think they would have let me commit bigamy."

● ● ● ● ●

Alafair didn't know how she felt. Disappointed that Pearl and Leon appeared to be in the clear. She sat in the buggy in front of Pearl's bungalow for a long time, halfway hoping that one or both of Dan's parents would notice her and come across the street to find out what she wanted. She badly wanted to question Dan's parents again, but after what Pearl had told her, she knew it would be futile for her to try. Still, Pearl had dropped a tidbit that Alafair wanted to pursue. Pearl's father, Bertram Evans, was thrilled about her upcoming marriage to Leon. Maybe he had been thrilled enough to do whatever brutal act was necessary to see that his daughter's wedding day occurred on schedule.

Pearl herself had been a surprise. No wilting flower, she—not at all the way she had appeared at the funeral. She could have persuaded someone to remove Dan for her. Pearl was certainly not the first woman Alafair had known who manipulated the men in her life by letting them think they were smarter and tougher than she was.

There was no time to follow up on it now. She would have to tell Lawyer Meriwether what she had discovered and leave it in his hands. She needed to get back to her children in Boynton, and then to Muskogee to be with Gee Dub. But she had one more stop to make before she went home.

Chapter Twenty-six

It took Alafair a moment to get her bearings when she parked her buggy at the white frame storefront standing between two empty lots. She had not been to Council Hill for quite some time and was shocked to see what had become of it.

She stood on the boardwalk with her hands on her hips as she took in the ruins of the town.

She had heard that a tornado struck here a couple of years earlier, but she had no idea it had wreaked such havoc. Council Hill had been an important rail junction for the local cattle farmers and was a going concern last time Alafair had come through. What was once a lively business district on the main street now had more vacant lots and boarded-up buildings than working establishments. The red brick Methodist Church that Alafair remembered was still standing, and the cattle pens near the railroad station had been reconstructed. The rest of the little town had been left to its own devices. She wound her mare's reins around a hitching ring in front of the one restaurant in town and walked over to the general store/post office to ask directions to the home of the late Harvey Stump.

The Stump house was located only two long blocks to the south of downtown, so Alafair left her mare hitched in front of the Westlake Restaurant and made her way on foot. Whatever damage the tornado had caused to the cozy residential street no longer showed. The people who lived on Oak Street must have rebuilt, for even though the houses and their little yards were neatly kept, there were no trees of any size on the entire block.

The Stump house was the nicest on the block, Mr. Case had told her, so Alafair stopped in front of a square, frame house that was twice as big as any other in the neighborhood. Which still didn't make it all that large, but Alafair expected it was a comfortable size for two retirees and their grown son. The postage-stamp front yard was bare of shrubbery, but the grass lawn, just beginning to green up, was mowed. On the covered porch, two empty planter pots sat on either side of the front door.

She stood in the middle of the dirt street for some minutes thoughtfully regarding the house. The sun was shining, a soft cool breeze was ruffling her skirt. Birds chittered in the bushes as a tabby cat strolled down the street, tail high, indifferent to any concerns but its own. The peaceful ambiance held no residue of the violence that had occurred on that street only days earlier.

A movement caught Alafair's attention, breaking the spell. A woman had come out of the neighboring house and was standing on the porch, watching her. Alafair strode toward the house as the neighbor woman came down the porch steps to meet her on the walk.

The woman was of indeterminate race, a gray braid hanging down her back and skin brown as leather. She was bony and weathered, but her movements were fluid. Alafair judged her age to be somewhere between fifty and one hundred. Her green-brown eyes crinkled when she greeted Alafair with a cheerful, "Howdy. What can I do for you? If you're a-looking for Harvey Stump, you ain't going to find him this side of eternity."

Alafair liked the woman immediately and smiled back. She introduced herself, then got to the point. "Are you the lady who spoke to the law on the day that Mr. Stump met his maker?"

"I am. You can call me Granny Murray. It was quite the event, it was. Them two lawmen come pounding on the door, all shocked-looking and out of breath. The fat one told me that Harvey got done in, and they wanted to know if I had heard a ruckus anytime over the past few hours. I had, I told them. I saw Harvey and a man I didn't know having a set-to right on his porch and Harvey was getting the worst of it. That was, oh, about dinnertime on Thursday last. But Harvey was sure alive when the stranger left, I told them that. If he was the one come back and killed Harvey later, I wouldn't know. Are you a friend of Harvey's?"

"No, not exactly. I know the family, though, and I'd like to piece together what happened to him." Alafair figured that answer was vague enough. She extended a hand.

Granny Murray may have been starved for company, or just a busybody. Either way, she was delighted to have the opportunity to tell the exciting tale to someone new. "You want to come inside and have a glass of tea?"

"I'd be obliged," Alafair said.

• • ● • •

Granny Murray's house was neat and clean, but stuffed to the gills with furniture and geegaws. Two canaries in a giant wicker birdcage sat in front of a side window, and three cats lounged on the arms and seats of overstuffed chairs. Alafair expected that the canaries lived in a perpetual state of anxiety. The minute she sat down she found herself with a cat in her lap.

Granny Murray came back into the room with tall glasses of sweet tea on a tray and set them on a side table. "Yes, I was mighty surprised to see anybody at all visit that house," she said, saving Alafair the trouble of resuming the interrogation. "Harvey was a nice man. A helpful neighbor when I needed one. But he kept to himself. Never did have much company. Certainly not no men."

Alafair shifted the fat feline in her lap and took a tea glass from the table. "Did you get a good look at the man Harvey was arguing with, Miz Murray?"

"Well, I seen him. He was dark-haired, had on a black hat. That's about all I could tell. My eyesight ain't that good. Nothing wrong with my hearing, though. The stranger didn't say anything, but Harvey shrieked like a stuck pig. There was scuffle, though it looked to me like the stranger was the one doing all the fighting. He poked Harvey a couple of good ones and then he left. Got on a chestnut horse and rode off. Harvey went back inside and I didn't see him no more."

Alafair took a breath. A black hat and a chestnut horse. No wonder Scott thought the description sounded too much like Gee Dub for comfort. Alafair leaned forward. "Miz Murray, did you see a young woman with dark hair, blue skirt, white shirt? I expect she would have come by a little earlier than the man."

Granny Murray's eyes narrowed as she thought back. "I didn't see anybody like that. I didn't come out of the house until I heard Harvey yelling. He could have had a whole parade of company up till then. No, he never had young women to come by. There was an old woman used to visit him regular. I seen her stop by his place maybe once a week. She never came that day, though. Not that I saw."

"Do you know who she was? What did she look like?" Alafair could hardly contain herself.

Granny picked up the tabby that was winding itself around her ankles and settled back in her chair, clearly enjoying herself. "Little old bit of a thing. Looked like a stiff wind would blow her over. Never met her. Harvey's mama and daddy passed while he was at the war, so I figured she was his grandma. I kind of liked Harvey. He helped me mend that fence in the back that got ripped up in the big storm. It laid there for nigh on two years because I didn't have the money or the muscle to do it myself. He was quiet, never went out much. I give him okra from my garden when I got too much. Never had visitors. But for his grandma."

"Did you tell Marshal Gundry and Mr. Tucker about this woman?"

"Who's that?"

"The lawmen who found Harvey's body," Alafair prompted, impatient.

"Well, now, they didn't ask about her. They just asked if I'd seen anything unusual over to Harvey's because he was dead. Him and the stranger getting into it with one another, that was unusual."

"Would you recognize the old woman if you saw her again?

"I surely would." Granny's answer didn't surprise Alafair. She had probably had her nose pressed to the window most of the time. "You suspect she has something to do with Harvey getting killed?" Granny asked.

Alafair was suddenly anxious to leave and deliver this new information to Scott or Meriwether or anyone who might find some way to use it for Gee Dub's defense. She came up with the first reasonable response to Granny Murray's question she could think of. "I don't know, Miz Murray, but if she was Harvey's grandma, she ought to be told what happened to him."

Chapter Twenty-seven

Alafair walked at a brisk pace back toward downtown, intending to immediately drive back to Boynton. She rounded the corner from Oak onto Main Street and paused mid-step when she caught sight of the man sitting in a cane-bottomed chair in front of the Westlake Restaurant. Right where her buggy was parked. He had leaned back and crossed his ankles over the top of the hitching post, his hands clasped together over his ample belly. She straightened and marched up the sidewalk, coming to a halt beside him.

Scott Tucker, town sheriff of Boynton, Oklahoma, and her cousin by marriage, lifted his hat enough to cut her a sidelong glance from under the brim. "I knew I recognized that gray mare. What are you doing here, Alafair?"

"I could ask the same of you, Scott. You don't have any authority down here."

Scott's lips thinned. "Neither do you. Shaw told me you went to Okmulgee. What in blazes do you think you're doing here?"

"Same as you, I reckon. I must say, I'm glad to see that you've finally decided to side with the family and look further into this sad affair."

If Scott was hurt by her attitude, it didn't show. "That's just what I figured on doing, but when I saw your rig, I thought I'd better find out what you're up to first. I went looking for you at Stump's house, but you weren't there."

"I just spent a half-hour talking to the neighbor lady. Y'all should have questioned her more closely, Scott. She told me that the man she knew as Harvey used to get regular visits from an old woman. I talked privately to Pearl Johnson this morning, too, before I left Okmulgee. And from things she told me I'm betting the old woman is Dan Johnson's mother, Scott. His folks knew he was here all the time."

Scott held up a hand to slow the flood of words. "Hang on, now. Why else do you think I am here? Lawyer Meriwether told Shaw it'd be a good idea to engage a private agent to do some extra digging, so I volunteered to take on the job. I was going to start by talking to the neighbors again, but since you've already stuck a toe in that pond, let's have a sit in this cafe and you tell me what you've come up with before I waste my time going over the same road."

The dinnertime regulars gave Alafair and Scott a cursory once-over when they took their seats at a corner table, but interest waned after the waitress took their order. Still, Alafair kept her voice low as she brought Scott up to speed.

Scott mulled over her information for a few minutes before he said, "Alafair, even if Dan Johnson's mother did know where he was living and visited him every week, I don't see what that has to do with Dan's murder. I'd be hard-pressed to believe that she's the one who shot him."

"No, but what I'm thinking is that if Dan's parents knew where he was, it's likely somebody else knew, as well. You need to ask them who else they told, Scott. Or maybe somebody followed Miz Johnson when she came for a visit, somebody who wasn't happy to find out that Dan was still alive."

They fell silent while the waitress set down their glasses of tea. Scott resumed the conversation after she went back into the kitchen to slice pie. "All right, Alafair. If Dan's folks knew he was alive and pretending to be somebody else, that's probably going to get them into some trouble for abetting a fugitive, at least. Maybe they did tell someone else where he was. I'll look into it. What you don't know is that Holly came to see me yesterday evening and told me that she and Gee Dub were both here in Council Hill on the day Dan died. That she hitchhiked down here from Boynton and she did speak to Dan. And after she left his house, Gee Dub showed up and found her sitting in this very cafe. She says that the two of them left Council Hill together and were in one another's company from then until she went back up to the house and talked to you."

Alafair's stomach fluttered. He had been here, after all. All her supposition and theorizing about who else besides Gee Dub might have shot Dan Johnson could come to nothing. She decided to put her own spin on the new information. "Well, that's good! If Johnson didn't die until after the two of them had left town and they were together from then on, then Holly is Gee Dub's alibi."

She could tell by Scott's expression that he was sorry to have to tell her that Gee Dub was still very much a suspect. "It could be that the gunshot the neighbor lady heard after Holly and Gee left wasn't the one that killed Johnson."

Alafair wasn't about to give up. "Granny Murray was the last person to see Dan Johnson alive, and she swore that he was still alive after his fight with the stranger."

"But was the stranger really Gee Dub? Sounds like he was. And if he was, did he go directly from Johnson's house to meet up with Holly here at this cafe? Or did he lurk about until Johnson was in his garage and out of sight and then finish him off in private? Or maybe the both of them are in cahoots and did the deed together."

"Scott, you are reaching…"

He held up a hand to silence her. "Maybe. But the prosecutor is going to ask the same questions. One of the reasons I came down today is to talk to the waitress here and see if she's the one who served them two. And if she is, what does she remember? Now, she could tell me something that'll make Gee Dub or Holly or the both of them look guilty," Scott warned. "It's possible that she'll tell me that Holly sat here for hours before Gee Dub showed up. Or that he came in before she did, or that they came in together. She might have overheard them plotting to do away with Johnson, or concocting a story to make one or the other of them look innocent. Are you sure you want to hear what she has to say?"

She was amazed he'd ask. "Of course I do."

"Then you have to promise not to say a word. I don't want you jumping in with leading questions, or trying to defend him."

"But, Scott…"

"But nothing. Be quiet or leave."

Ruth Tucker had never visited anyone in the county jail before, and the fact that a matron insisted on patting her down before she was allowed to see Gee Dub didn't do anything to calm her nerves. Her fiancé, Trent Calder, had warned her how it was going to go before the two of them ever boarded the train for Muskogee, so she had already stiffened her resolve and determined to put up with whatever indignities were required. In truth, the matron's search was perfunctory, just checking the pockets in Ruth's skirt and looking in her handbag. Besides, Trent gave her a supportive smile when she emerged from the ladies' cloakroom and that made her feel much better. They had been briefed on protocol before they were led to the visitor's room, a basic affair with a bare table and four bare chairs and a uniformed guard standing at the door. They were to stay on their side of the table and not touch the prisoner nor give him anything. The guard was there to see that the rules were followed, but he didn't seem to be particularly interested in eavesdropping on their conversation. Ruth figured that if they kept their voices low, the guard wouldn't be able to overhear very much, if anything.

Ruth was surprised to see that Gee Dub looked fine. She suspected that if she were the one arrested on suspicion of murder, she would be so weak with fear that she would hardly be able to stand on her own two feet. But Gee Dub seemed rested and calm.

Why that was, she couldn't say, but she hoped it was because he was confident that he would be cleared of suspicion shortly. After what he had been through in France, he probably didn't find incarceration particularly troubling. His attitude lifted her spirits, even in light of what she and Trent had come to tell him. Her first words to Gee Dub after he sat down were innocuous enough. "How are they treating you, Gee?"

One corner of his mouth lifted. "Couldn't be better," he said. "How are things at home?"

"About the same. Everybody is worried about you, of course. Listen, Gee Dub, Holly went to talk to Scott yesterday evening, and Trent heard it all."

The door between the front office and the jail cells stood open while Holly was telling her story to Scott. Trenton Calder had been in an open cell sitting on a cot with his hands clasped between his knees, listening to every word of the conversation.

Trent related what Holly had said, his voice low, aware of the guard at the door. Gee Dub Tucker listened attentively, one elbow on the table and his cheek propped on his fist.

"What did you do after Holly left the farm, Gee Dub?" Ruth asked, after Trent finished his tale. "Scott has already told Lawyer Meriwether everything that Holly said. Daddy and Mr. Meriwether will be by this afternoon and I'm sure they'll ask you all about it."

Gee Dub sighed, but didn't change positions. There was no use trying to keep Holly's name out of it now. "I knew she would go to Council Hill. She was already at Johnson's place when I got there. I waited round the corner till she left Johnson's house."

"Did you talk to Johnson?"

"Well, after she left, I did go up to the house."

Trent straightened. "What were you thinking?"

A moment's pause. "I was looking out for Holly."

"What did you say to him?"

"Nothing."

Trent had a sour feeling in his gut. Gee Dub was not only his beloved Ruth's older brother, he had been Trent's best friend for years. The war had changed them both, but Trent was overcome by a sinking suspicion that it had changed Gee Dub out of all recognition. He asked again. "What did you do, Gee?"

Gee Dub dropped his hand and turned his head enough to regard Trent with one eye. His expression had hardened. "I punched him in the face."

Ruth looked as though she wanted to cry. "Did you kill him?"

"He was plenty alive when I left. It took me a while to figure out where Holly had gone, but I finally spotted her in that restaurant on the main street."

Ruth sighed with relief. If her brother said it was so, then it was so.

Trent felt his shoulders relax, as well. Gee Dub had never been a liar. But he said, "Gee Dub, this looks bad."

Gee Dub gave him a dry smile. "You reckon?"

Chapter Twenty-eight

The waitress at the Westlake Restaurant was only too happy to tell Scott everything she knew about the crying woman and tall man who had sat at this very table on the day Harvey Stump was killed. The woman introduced herself as Joan McNamara, proprietress, as round and brown and fragrant as one of her loaves of fresh bread.

Once Scott had explained his mission to her, Joan called a younger woman—her daughter, judging by the look of her—from the kitchen to take over service. Joan took a chair between the lawman and the dark-haired woman with the flushed face and unhappy expression, who nodded at her but said nothing.

"Do you think those young folks had something to do with Harvey Stump's murder?" Joan's eyes were wide with speculation.

"That's what we're here to find out," Scott said.

Scott kept his tone and manner as discreet as possible while he questioned Joan, though he was pretty certain that everything he said would be common knowledge around Council Hill within minutes after he and Alafair left town. He wasn't too bothered by that fact. Once the gossip mill spread the word, anyone who thought he knew anything about the death of Harvey Stump/Dan Johnson would eagerly come forward.

The story Joan told fit in well with the tale that Holly had related to Scott. Joan didn't know the name of the woman who had come into the cafe that day, but she was very small and thin, with hair the color of dark honey. She had wept like her heart was broken. She told Joan that someone she loved once had died. Alafair made a surprised noise when the waitress said that, and Scott shot her a stern glance before nodding at Joan to continue.

"The little gal wanted to know about the next train to Boynton, but the last one that day had already been through. She didn't want to wait for the morning one, though. I didn't ask what she aimed to do with herself and she didn't say. She said she could eat something, and by the time I brought it out, this young fellow was sitting in that chair there, right next to her. She had started crying again so I figured he was bothering her. But she said he was a friend. He was a nice-looking youngster. They sat here together and grazed on this and that and talked for, oh, about an hour. Then they left together. He was on a chestnut mare and she rode astride behind his saddle. I didn't see which way they went after that."

Scott nodded. "How long was the woman here before her friend came in?"

"Not long. Fifteen minutes, maybe?"

Scott allowed himself to feel a little bit relieved. He glanced at Alafair. She was about to chew off her bottom lip. He started to ask Joan if she was sure, but Joan volunteered some observations of her own.

"Harvey Stump used to eat here every once in a while," she said. "He seemed like a nice enough fellow. I knew his folks, you know. They just moved into town not six months before they both died of the grippe. They were lovely people. They told me that Champlin struck oil on their little farm south of here and they were able to buy a nice house here in town that didn't require much upkeep."

"So they had money." Scott made the observation aloud. "I don't suppose they ever told you where they did their banking, did they, Miz McNamara?"

Joan's eyes widened. "Well, no, neither of them ever mentioned. Mr. Stump did say they were right happy that they were never going to be a burden to their boy, and they were going to be able to leave him well off when their time came. I'm sure he had no idea how soon his time would come. I was real sorry that Harvey never got home from Europe in time to see them before they passed. His daddy was real proud of his soldier boy. And now Harvey got shot. It's just a tragedy."

Alafair couldn't contain herself. She gripped Scott's arm and whispered an urgent question into his ear. Scott would have been annoyed if it hadn't been such a good question. He turned to Joan. "Did Harvey ever come in here with an older woman, maybe looked like his grandma?"

"No. I never saw Harvey with anybody. I heard that he didn't have any family left after his mama and daddy died. So sad. I wish I had made more of an effort to be neighborly. But you can imagine, this eatery keeps me pretty busy. I never did even know where Harvey lived."

"Over on Oak Street," Scott told her.

"Oak Street?" Joan blinked. "Now, you said Harvey got killed the same day that young couple were here?"

"Yes, later that night, we think."

"There was somebody else stopped by here that evening, another stranger. I remember because we don't usually get that many strangers in one day. He asked if I knew where Oak Street was."

Alafair forgot all about her vow of silence. "It was a man? Was he riding a quarter horse with a blaze?"

Joan looked at her, surprised to hear her speak at last. "Yes, a man. But I didn't see that he was riding anything."

Scott put a hand on Alafair's arm before he said, "Can you describe him, Miz McNamara?"

"Dressed real nice, like a man of substance, that's what I noticed right away. He had on a black suit and a black homburg. I asked him if he wanted a table but he said he was looking for Oak Street. He never said anything about Harvey Stump, though. Maybe it was just a coincidence."

"A young man?"

"Well, no, not so young. Not all that old, either. Maybe forty-five?"

Alafair was squirming like her chair was on fire. Scott was doing his best to ignore her. "And this fellow never said his name to you, Miz McNamara?"

"Never did. He looked to be an upstanding citizen, though, so I never thought twice about giving him directions."

• • ● • •

"Scott, it's Pearl Johnson's daddy, I know it is!" The accusation burst from Alafair like a shot fired the minute she and Scott stepped out of the cafe and onto the street.

"Now, Alafair, you don't know that. You don't know that the man had anything to do with Dan Johnson at all. He might have just been a salesman looking for some business. None of Johnson's neighbors that I talked to ever said anything about seeing a well-dressed man at the house."

"It was late in the evening when Granny Murray heard the shot, though, so maybe none of the neighbors were outside to see anybody. Are you going to go to Okmulgee now and question Mr. Evans?"

"I'm going to talk to Dan Johnson's neighbors again, Alafair, and you are going to go home."

"You already talked to the neighbors, you and that Marshal Gundry."

"I know that you're champing at the bit to prove Gee Dub innocent, but this is not the way to go about it. I'll follow up on what Miz McNamara said, but right now…"

She spoke over him. "There's no time to waste going over old ground. If you don't aim to go to Okmulgee right now and talk to Bertram Evans, I will."

Scott bit his words off in surprise. "No, you will not."

She placed her hands on her hips. "How are you going to stop me?"

"I could arrest you for interfering with an investigation."

That seemed to amuse her. "You're not going to clap me in jail. Besides, you said yourself that you've got no authority here."

"Isn't Shaw expecting you home?"

"I'll send him a wire."

Scott's face was getting very red. "I ought to haul you back up to Boynton by the scruff of your neck and hand you over to Shaw. Let him deal with you."

"Shaw would agree with me."

Scott had to stop himself from saying a bad word. She was right. Even if he managed to wrestle Alafair back to Boynton and remand her to her husband's custody, his cousin Shaw Tucker probably would be on her side. The two had always functioned more as a unit than as individuals, and it was their son who was in peril, after all. It was more likely that the moment his back was turned, Shaw and Alafair would race to Okmulgee and confront Bertram Evans together. Then Scott would have to deal with both of them, and Shaw would not be nearly as easy to manhandle as Alafair.

Scott was sputtering, but he had not come up with a rejoinder. Alafair sensed victory. "So we can go to Okmulgee right now? I'll board my horse in yon livery stable and ride with you in your automobile. It shouldn't take us but two or three hours to get there. I promise won't say a word while you're talking to Mr. Evans."

Scott sighed. "Alafair, you are the most exasperating human person on this green Earth."

Chapter Twenty-nine

Scott and Alafair had not spoken much to one another on the way to Okmulgee. Scott was still annoyed and Alafair knew better than to say anything that might make him reconsider their agreement. They arrived in Okmulgee late in the afternoon, so Scott thought it was wiser to look for Mr. Evans at his office on the second floor of the First National Bank Building. Alafair followed him up the stairs, but stood just outside the open door to Evans' office, in the hall, trying to remain invisible and at the same time hear everything that was said. She would have found a way to barge her way in if Scott had managed to get an interview with Evans. But as it turned out, Mr. Evans had gone home early. Scott had to show the secretary his round tin badge in order to pry Evans' address out of him. The constable's badge from the town of Boynton didn't mean anything in Okmulgee. It hardly meant anything five feet outside of the Boynton town limits. But it seemed to do the trick.

Scott parked his Paige at the edge of the shady street and he and Alafair walked up the long graveled drive leading to a two-story native stone manse with white columns running along the front of the deep, wraparound porch. Bertram Evans' construction business was apparently doing very well.

Alafair had made the twenty-five-mile trip in an open conveyance over the unpaved road between Council Hill and Okmulgee twice in one day. She was feeling gritty and rattled and expected that she did not present an impressive figure, with windblown tendrils of dark hair falling into her face and her second-best hat with the cherries on the band slipping askew on her head no matter how many times she readjusted her hatpin.

Still, she would have insisted on coming along to question Evans even if she had just crawled through a twenty-five-mile mudhole on her belly.

Scott gave her a once-over before knocking on the door. The determined expression on her dusty face both amused him and made him want to shake her by the shoulders. He did think that this entire escapade was going to make a great story to tell his wife, Hattie. "You remember your promise, now, Alafair," he warned. "You can come along and listen, but I'm asking the questions."

She didn't look at him. Her gaze was boring a hole in the side of the house. "I remember," she said, just as a servant in a white apron opened the door.

• • ● • •

Alafair could not remember ever having been in such a magnificent house. The servant left them standing in a grand foyer with an even grander staircase that ascended and wound around to form a mezzanine on the second floor. A marble table in the middle of the foyer seemed to have no function other than to hold a huge arrangement of purple irises and white hyacinth. The fragrance was overwhelming.

The maid reappeared in the entryway to the left and said, "Come this way, please." She led them down a window-lined hall to a tall set of double doors, which she opened with great ceremony before standing aside.

Bertram Evans was seated behind a mahogany desk to their left. He stood to greet them when they entered. Two women were ensconced in wing chairs in front of a marble fireplace at the end of the room. The younger woman leaned forward in her chair and gave Alafair an ironic grin.

"Well, look who's here, Daddy," said Pearl Johnson.

Scott would have much preferred to speak to Mr. Evans on his own, but Mrs. Evans and Pearl stayed where they were and Evans did not try to shift them. Scott didn't fault the man. He couldn't get Alafair to leave, either.

Following introductions, Evans escorted his guests to a long couch in front of the fireplace, all the easier for his wife and daughter to hear from their armchairs. Evans himself sat down on an ottoman at his wife's feet. One might be forgiven for thinking Evans had put himself at a disadvantage by taking such a humble seat, but Scott saw the move for what it was. This was a man who felt no need to resort to posturing in order to demonstrate his superiority.

Pearl had already told her parents about Alafair's visit early that morning, so there was no need to cover old ground. It took several minutes for Scott to relate all the new information he and Alafair had uncovered. The Evans family listened quietly, and to Scott's relief, Alafair said nothing, either.

After the story of the trip to Council Hill was finished, Scott paused, waiting to hear if Evans had anything to say before Scott began posing questions.

Evans turned on his footstool to look at his wife.

"He thinks you are the man in the black suit, Bertram," Mrs. Evans said to her husband. Her tone was unemotional. "He's wondering if you killed Dan."

"So I gather." He turned back toward Scott. "It was not I who shot Dan, Mr. Tucker. I hated the bas…the rat. I was glad to hear that he died and that my daughter was free of him." He cast a glance at Pearl. She did not look upset. She was familiar with her father's opinion of Dan Johnson. Evans continued. "I did not even know he was alive until after he really did die. If I had known, I might have thought about taking the easy road and getting rid of him for Pearl's sake. But I would not have done it because I would not want to complicate things for Pearl or for my wife, either. No, I didn't kill him. In fact, the man in the black suit could not have been me because on the twenty-fourth day of last month through the twenty-eighth, my wife and I were in Oklahoma City. I had business to conduct in the city, and we took the opportunity to visit with my wife's sister while we were there. We stayed with my sister-in-law while we were in town. I will be glad to give you a list of a dozen people who will be able to vouch for our whereabouts during that entire week."

Alafair shifted in her seat, but kept her peace.

"When did you hear that Dan had been killed, Mr. Evans?" Scott said.

"Not until we returned home late on the twenty-eighth."

Scott's eyes narrowed and he looked at Pearl. "Miz Johnson, you didn't send your mother and father a wire with the news when you found out your late husband had not actually been dead all that time?"

"No, I didn't. What would have been the point? I knew it would upset them, and like it says in the Bible, 'sufficient unto the day is the evil thereof.' Besides, I not only had to deal with Leon, I was worried about what the news would do to Dan's mother. I half-expected her to drop dead on the spot."

"Were y'all aware that Johnson's mother knew he was living in Council Hill all along?" Scott directed the question to the room.

"I don't believe it," Pearl said.

Evans was not quite so taken aback. "Is that so? What makes you think that?"

Alafair felt fairly confident that Scott was not going to throw her out of the room, so she said, "Miz Johnson was seen by the neighbors. Several times." She didn't mention that at this point there was no firm proof that the elderly woman the neighbor saw was indeed Dan's mother.

Mrs. Evans didn't require proof. "Well, I'm not surprised," she said. "Poor Lucy would walk over coals for that boy, not that he deserved her loyalty. But a mother will do anything to protect her children. Won't she, Miz Tucker?"

Scott did not give Alafair time to respond. He stood up, and so did everyone else. "Mr. Evans, ladies, I want to thank you for taking the time to talk to us. I will report what you told me to the defendant's lawyer and I'm sure he will be in touch."

"We'll be available," Evans said.

Mrs. Evans picked up a little bell from the side table and rang it. "Minnie will show you out." She extended a hand to Alafair. "Good luck."

Chapter Thirty

Alafair nearly trod on Scott's heels as he strode down the long drive to the street where he had parked his Paige. "Who could the man in the black suit be if it isn't Evans and it isn't Leon? What can we do now?"

Scott did not slow down. "Meriwether will want to check up on Evans' story. Until he can do that, I reckon I'd better drop in on Chief Bowman and bring him up to speed. Evans may not have gone to Council Hill himself, but he could have hired him an assassin. Bowman might want to keep an eye on the Evanses, here, make sure they don't skip town."

"Before you do, can't we go see Dan's parents one more time?"

"Why? Surely you don't think Dan's mother will say anything that would help exonerate the man she thinks killed her son."

"Does she think that, Scott? Does she really think Gee Dub killed Dan? You heard what Miz Evans said. Us mothers understand one another. If Miz Johnson was to see what I'm trying to do, she might be more willing talk to us. To tell us what she knows of Dan's life in Council Hill, tell us who else may have known he was there. Besides, from the look of her I don't think she's going to last much longer. What if she goes to her reward before we find out if she knows something that could help Gee Dub?"

They were halfway down the Evanses' driveway when Scott stopped walking and turned around so abruptly that Alafair nearly ran into him. "That poor woman has had a bitter cup to drink, Alafair, and I don't relish adding more poison to it. Let her die in peace."

"What harm can it do her now to tell the truth? It will be a blessing to help her unburden her soul." Alafair was reaching, and she knew it. Scott drew a breath to tell her so, but she didn't give him the chance. "Scott, it's for Gee Dub. Any little piece of information may be the key. What if it was one of your boys who was in Gee Dub's spot? What if it was Spike?"

That made Scott pause. His youngest boy, Spike, was only twenty years old and determined to cause his parents heartache and worry. Still smarting because, even though he joined up as soon as he was old enough, he was never sent overseas, and he was unreasonably angry at his mother and father for being relieved.

Alafair was driving Scott around the bend with her unwavering tenacity and her refusal to see reason, and worse, her absolute certainty that she was right. He didn't know why he was letting it bother him. She had always been this way, as long as he had known her, at least. More than once in the past he had taken advantage of the fact that people were willing to tell Alafair things that they would never think of telling him. A slight, brown, middle-aged mother of ten may have seemed like a threat to no one, but that was a dangerous misconception. To protect her children, Alafair was all teeth and claws.

"All right, gol-durn it. We can go by the Johnson house for a minute. But she don't have to talk to either of us if she don't want to," Scott warned.

• • ● ● •

The day was well along and the shadows deep by the time Alafair and Scott reached the Johnson house.

Alafair stood back while Scott knocked. Fern Johnson answered. "Not you again," he said, but he didn't slam the door in their faces, which Scott took as a good sign.

Still, he wasn't going to take any chances. He said, "Mr. Johnson, I'm sorry to bedevil you, but a man's life is on the line. When I wired you that your son had died of the flu outside of

Boynton, did y'all already know the dead man was not Dan? Did y'all know that Dan was alive? That he had stolen Harvey Stump's life and was living in Council Hill?"

Mr. Johnson's eyebrows flew toward his hairline. "What? No. What kind of a question is that?"

Scott gestured toward Alafair, preparing to introduce her, but Mr. Johnson turned away when his wife's thin voice called from the parlor, "Fern, let him in."

Johnson disappeared, leaving Scott and Alafair on the porch. They could hear the low murmur of voices inside the house. Johnson sounded distressed. Mrs. Johnson sounded resigned. Alafair was watching the screen door like it was a snake poised to strike. Scott was watching Alafair. One by one, people were falling off of her list of alternative suspects and her worry was written on her face. Scott wondered himself what he would to do next if none of their new leads paid off. Talk to Chief Bowman at the Okmulgee Police Department, as he had told Alafair. Go back to Council Hill and make the rounds of Dan Johnson's neighbors yet again. But his first job would be to get Alafair out of his hair. His compassion for her situation was real, but her fierce determination to prove Gee Dub innocent was beginning to affect him. She would not entertain the thought that her son might actually be guilty. Scott could not afford to abandon his objectivity.

Scott was so lost in his own thoughts that he flinched when Johnson opened the screen and stepped out onto the porch.

"My wife wants to talk to you while she still can." Johnson did not look happy. "Lucy is near the end and I do not expect her to live but a few more days. So I'm warning you, if you upset her unnecessarily I will report you to the police and have you barred from speaking to us again."

"I understand," Scott said.

Johnson stood aside and Scott preceded him into the house, but when Alafair took a step forward, Johnson blocked her with an arm. "Who are you? You came to the house with Charles Tucker and his wife after Dan's funeral."

A salty word crossed Alafair's mind. She had hoped to remain invisible and anonymous for as long as possible. There was no getting around it now. "My name is Alafair Tucker. I am cousin to Scott Tucker and the mother of the man falsely accused of murdering Dan."

She half-expected Johnson to toss her off the porch on her ear. Instead he sagged, defeated. "Oh, Lord Jesus," he murmured.

• • ● • •

Lucy Johnson had shrunk to almost nothing in the few days since Scott saw her last. If Johnson hadn't told him that his wife was at death's door, Scott would have known it after one look. There was hardly any body left to contain her soul. She was seated on one of the wingback armchairs beside the settee, wrapped chin to toe in several quilts and blankets. A hand-knit wool cap on her head was pulled down almost to her eyebrows. If it hadn't been for the gray, skull-like little face peeking out from all the coverings, one would never know there was a person in the chair.

Her gaze went immediately to Alafair. "Your son is the young man they have in jail up in Muskogee?" Her voice was weak and papery.

Alafair knelt down on the floor in front of the other mother and put gentle hands on her knees. "I am. But I know my boy did not kill your boy, Miz Johnson. Surely the most important thing is to be sure that Dan's true killer is brought to justice. My son had no reason on Earth to harm Dan. He was just in the wrong place at the wrong time. All I want in the world is to clear his name and find out who really shot Dan."

Scott was impressed. He knew that Alafair didn't care in the least who shot Dan Johnson as long as she could save Gee Dub. But one would never know it from her sincere delivery. Scott didn't think Lucy was fooled, but that didn't seem to matter. She listened impassively while Alafair spoke, then drew a shaky breath before she said, "Miz Tucker, I don't know if your son killed my Dan or not. I hope, for your sake, he did not. There is no pain like losing a child."

"I do know, Miz Johnson, I do. And there is nothing that will make that pain better but time. Even then...."

"I have no time. But I do have the knowledge that I will be reunited with my boy directly."

Considering the way Dan Johnson had conducted his life, Alafair wasn't entirely sure that was so. But she said, "Praise the Lord. Still, there is no room in the heaven-bound heart for vengeance. What we must seek is true justice."

Scott was standing quietly by the front door, interested to see where Alafair was going with this.

Lucy looked up at him. "Mr. Tucker, I don't see how it will help the investigation, but if there is a slim chance that I can provide you with some clue that will help you find out who killed my boy, even if it is this lady's son, I will tell you what I know. Besides, it's high time I unburden myself. "

Fern Johnson frowned. "Mother, you'll just tire yourself out. What can you possibly say...?"

Lucy ignored him. "Yes, I knew Dan was alive."

Alafair sat back on her heels and Mr. Johnson made an unintelligible noise. Lucy continued. "Fern had no idea Dan was alive, Sheriff Tucker. Not then. I was the only one who knew that it wasn't him buried up in Boynton. Dan came to Okmulgee back in December, snuck into town and came to the house while Fern was at work. He told me that when his dad wired him that I was sick, he requested leave to come home. But before his leave was granted, he got in a fight, and the other man fell and hit his head and died. So Dan ran away. He was afraid that if he got arrested, if he stood trial and went to prison, he'd never be able to get home and see me before I pass over Jordan. He traveled a ways with this fellow Harvey Stump, but then Harvey died of the grippe and all of a sudden Dan had the means to start a new life. He begged me not to tell his father that he was alive. I should have. I should have told Dan to do the right thing and pay for his mistakes. But I couldn't do it. He was my child and I couldn't stand to see his life ruined. As best I could, I helped him set himself up as Harvey Stump. He never told me he had married that other woman in New England, but he did say that he wanted to let Pearl go so she could find a better husband. I told him when she got engaged to the Stryker boy, and he said he was happy for her."

Scott thought it was suspicious that Dan had benefited so handily from a couple of mighty convenient deaths. The way that Dan had manipulated his mother did not sit well, either. "Miz Johnson, he was living so close. It would have been easy for somebody who knew him as Dan to pass through Council Hill and recognize him. Didn't it cross your mind that someday he'd be found out and poor Pearl's second marriage would be null and void?"

Lucy's lips twitched. "Mr. Tucker, a lot of things crossed my mind in the three months Dan was in Council Hill. But he was just staying there temporarily. I'd already told him to head for Mexico as soon as I quit coming to see him. I never told another soul where he was, so there was no other way to let him know when I pass. I was so upset after you and that dark-haired girl came looking for him. I was afraid that you would find him out then, but when I made it over to Council Hill to warn him, he told me not to worry. He said you had no idea who it was that you buried and there was no way you could find out. Dan had taken all the identification off of Harvey's body and replaced it with his own. So how could you possibly figure out that Dan Johnson had become Harvey Stump?

"So I felt better, then. Until a few days later, Fern told me that you had traced the dead man's name through something you found in his pocket before you buried him. I knew Dan was caught then, and I would have driven over to warn him. But that was a bad day. The pain was so bad I could hardly stand. I didn't have any choice but to tell my husband that Dan had been living in Council Hill all the time."

Mr. Johnson had taken a seat in a kitchen chair by his wife's side, and Lucy's head slowly, slowly turned to give him a tender look. "Fern was terribly upset with me, but I told him how Dan had taken a God-given chance to make up for all his sins. To make up for all the years of grief he'd given us. He was doing it, too. Fern would be so proud of the man Dan had become. He was helping his neighbors and going to church and all. It would have been a tragedy if he had gotten arrested. I begged Fern to go to Council Hill and help Dan escape. He called Miz Clay to come over and stay with me that evening and rode over to Council Hill. I was on pins and needles until Fern came home. I knew I'd never set eyes on my son again, but I was so relieved when Fern told me that Dan was leaving Council Hill that very night. Dan told his daddy he'd contact us somehow when he got settled in Mexico. But you already know what happened instead. He never made it out of town. He got ambushed and shot dead before he could get away. When Chief Bowman came here the next day to tell us that our son had been murdered, I would have died right then and there if it hadn't been for Fern. Our poor son. I've cried more tears over my child than any mother ought to. Dan will never break another heart, and soon I will have no more tears, no more pain, no more sorrow." She shifted in her chair to face Alafair. "I'm not long for this world, and I expect that in the next world I'll have to pay for what I did. All I wanted was to protect my son. You should understand that."

Mr. Johnson put his arm around his wife's shoulder. "That's enough, Mother. Try not to fret yourself any more. Come and lie down, now. There is nothing else you need to say." He helped Lucy to her feet and carefully supported her as they walked back to the bedroom. Scott and Alafair sat in silence until Johnson returned several minutes later.

He took a seat in a vacant armchair. "She's asleep now."

"Mr. Johnson," Scott said, "when you went to Council Hill to warn Dan that night, did you stop at the cafe on Main and ask for directions to Oak Street?"

"I did."

Alafair looked at Scott, confused. Fern Johnson was the man in the black suit?

Scott's expression was unreadable. "Mr. Johnson, did you shoot your son?"

Johnson leaned back, crossed his legs, and sighed deeply. "I wondered how long it would take for somebody to figure it out. My wife doesn't know I shot him, or pretends not to. From the way she talked to Miz Tucker, I reckon she has an idea. I didn't tell her, at least. It was an accident, Sheriff."

Alafair gasped. She had hoped that the Johnsons might provide a lead that would help clear Gee Dub. This was not at all what she expected.

Johnson sighed again. "It happened like Lucy said. Dan told no one but his mother about his new life as Harvey Stump. She kept a good secret, too, because I sure thought he was dead and buried. When she finally had to come out with it, I told her I would drive over there and warn him. I was really aiming to force him to turn himself in. I never wanted to hurt her, but she's spent her life protecting that boy from the consequences of his bad behavior. The only way he was ever going to really get a fresh start in life was to come clean and finally drink the bitter cup of justice to the dregs.

"Lucy gave me pretty good directions and I recognized the house once I found out where Oak Street was. Nobody answered when I knocked, so I went inside and looked around. He had packed his gear. He had already found out that the law was on to him and he was getting ready to hit the road. I didn't know it then, but that very day he had met with Miz Thornberry and she had already let the cat out of the bag. I found him in the garage, sporting a black eye, with a steamer trunk in the back of his auto and a tote full of money. He was mighty shocked to see me, especially when I told him I wasn't going to let him get away again.

"His mother thinks he changed, but he didn't. He might have spent a few minutes considering the noble idea of atonement, but when it came right up to it, he didn't have the spine. I asked him why he risked staying in Council Hill so long. He said it was because of his ma, and besides, it took a while for all of Stump's inheritance to get through probate court.

"I think when Harvey Stump offered to pay his way home, Dan decided he could kill two birds with one stone—see his mother one last time, and talk her into giving him enough money to get to Mexico. Then Stump died, and he came up with a better plan. He laughed when I pointed the rifle at him. 'You ain't going to shoot me, Pa,' he said. He was right. I wouldn't have. But when he laughed at me I saw red. I aimed to fire at the wall behind him, put the fear of God in him. He must have seen it in my eyes, the fury for all the years of misery he put us through, because he grabbed the rifle by the barrel. I expect he meant to jerk it away from me. But it went off."

Johnson leaned forward suddenly, doubled up with pain, his head over his knees as though he had been punched. He emitted a sob, and Alafair had to stop herself from reaching out to put a hand on his back. She glanced at Scott. He did not appear to be particularly sympathetic to the man's agony.

Johnson pulled himself together and sat up. "He lived long enough to say 'Don't tell Ma.'" He pressed his hands over his eyes. "He really did love his mother, in his way."

"Mr. Johnson," Scott said, "if it was an accident, why did you not come forward? And why not come forward when you heard that a man had been arrested? Did you intend to let Miz Tucker's son go to prison for a homicide he did not commit?"

Johnson was looking at Alafair when he answered Scott's question. "I wouldn't have let your son go to prison. I'm sorry you've had to go through this. But Lucy cannot live another week. I wanted to spare her the knowledge that I had killed our son. I wanted her to go to heaven believing that he really had changed, that she had not wasted a lifetime of love on an unworthy son."

Chapter Thirty-one

It was long after suppertime when Alafair and Scott showed up on Charles Tucker's doorstep. The idea of driving back to Boynton from Okmulgee in the dark didn't appeal to either one of them. After all her hours of hard travel and her emotional exhaustion, Alafair could have sworn the day had been at least twice as long as normal.

Lavinia and Charles were more than happy to put them up for the night. Aside from the fact that they were kin, they had a riveting story to share. Scott telephoned his wife, Hattie, and asked her to inform the family that they'd be back in the morning, after a detour to Council Hill to retrieve Alafair's horse and buggy. Alafair took the opportunity to have a bath and a change of clothes before Lavinia had a supper of leftovers ready for her guests.

Once the four of them were arranged around Lavinia's mahogany dining table, Scott managed to talk and wolf down his sandwich at the same time. "After he confessed, Johnson telephoned his lawyer to meet us at the police station. Then he walked next door to the neighbor's house and asked the lady to come sit with his wife while he went to turn himself in. He even took the rifle that shot Dan to give to Chief Bowman."

Charles shook his head, amazed at the turn of events. "What do you suppose will happen to him?"

"Well, that's up to the District Attorney over in Muskogee County." Scott paused long enough to let Lavinia fill his iced tea glass from the pitcher. "But I wouldn't be surprised if he got off pretty light."

Lavinia looked up from refreshing Alafair's drink. "Will Gee Dub be released now?"

"Chief Bowman sent the wire to the District Attorney's office while we were there," Scott said. "The boy will likely be back in Boynton by the time we get home."

"I must say, Alafair, you should be walking on air right now."

"Well, I am, Lavinia. I'm so relieved that I can barely stand up. But I can't help but feel sorry for Dan's parents."

"Now, you do surprise me, Alafair," Charles said. "If the mother hadn't tried so hard to protect that scalawag son and the daddy hadn't tried to so hard to protect her, this whole mess would never have happened."

Alafair didn't reply to Charles' observation. She didn't want to say right out loud that if she could have she would have done the same and worse to protect Gee Dub, or any one of her children. Instead, she turned to Scott. "Thank you for not giving up, Scott, no matter how bad it looked for Gee Dub."

Scott smiled. "Well, of course. No matter what happens, we Tuckers have to stick together."

• • ● ● •

After Gee Dub finally got home from Muskogee, there was a giant family celebration at his grandparents' farm, where he endured the hugs and congratulations of his entire extended family and ate from a spread that would have fed his old regiment. Alice had brought Holly to the welcome home party, but she and Gee Dub didn't say much to one another. They simply exchanged a few knowing looks, and that was enough. Private Moretti hung around in a corner and said nothing at all. When the party ended, Holly went home with Alice. Gee Dub made his way to his solitary room at the back of the toolshed and slept for twenty hours. The next morning he went up to the house long enough to let his mother fix breakfast for him and briefly discuss the future with his father. He and Private Moretti and Charlie Dog spent the rest of that day in the woods behind the farmhouse, doing nothing but walking among the trees. The grapevines were budding and little white flowers were poking up through the litter on the ground. What peace there was here. It was likely that the mockingbird would raise her family under the eaves of the toolshed undisturbed.

Everything was fine. This strange state of being was so fragile that Gee Dub was almost afraid to breathe for fear of ruining it.

Moretti followed Gee Dub along the well-trodden path the family had used for years to traverse the woods on the way to Grandma and Grandpapa's house. They didn't speak for a long time, but Gee Dub was well aware of Moretti's presence.

They came to a place in the woods that was fairly clear of brush yet canopied over by the budding branches of hickory, elm, and burr oak. A wild grapevine as thick as a man's wrist looped down off of the branches of an ancient oak, forming a natural swing that the Tucker siblings had taken full advantage of when they were children. And still did, truth be told. Gee Dub sat down in the grapevine swing and spent a moment watching Moretti and the dog wander through the clearing.

"You know, Moretti, it took me a while to remember just how it happened. I even got it in my head that you might have done Johnson in. But of course that's not the way it happened. If it hadn't been for you, I'd have killed him."

Moretti looked up from his handful of last year's acorns. "Yes, sir. I know."

Gee Dub sat in his swing and looked at Moretti for…he didn't know how long, exactly. Quite a long time. Finally he said, "You ought to go home, Private. It's time to try and let go of the war."

"I doubt if that can be done, Lieutenant."

Gee Dub smiled. "Well, yes, I guess that is wishful thinking on my part. Still, maybe it's time for you to finally meet my folks."

"Yes sir, Mr. Tucker, I think it is."

Chapter Thirty-two

Gee Dub stood gazing out the one small window of the bunk room with his back to the people who were seated at the painted table. It seemed easier not to look at them, not to see judgment in their eyes. He had invited his parents to come to his room rather than bring Moretti to the house. He felt more in control in his own space, and he didn't want other ears to hear.

He could feel their eyes boring into his back. It was deathly quiet in the room, not even a spring breeze fluttering the curtains. He wondered if his parents were both holding their breath, waiting for him to begin. He had a feeling that Alafair knew what he was going to say. Moretti's knapsack, the one Phoebe had found, was on the table in front of her. She had brought it with her.

He clasped his hands behind his back and began. "Private Moretti was in my outfit when we first went over to France. I never saw anybody so clumsy in my life, but he sure aimed to please. He had a sweet nature, but he couldn't hit the floor if he fell out of bed. The other boys figured he was their good luck charm, like a mascot. If somebody as useless as Moretti could keep from getting killed, then staying alive would be a piece of cake for the rest of them. Anyway, I knew how the boys felt, so I kind of made Moretti my project. I figured if I kept an eye on him and kept him from wandering into a bullet, that'd be good for morale, if nothing else.

"It worked, for a while, anyway. We were behind the lines for the first few weeks, scouting, mostly, and running supplies up the line. Those French towns…The soldiers on both sides who had been in France for years, well, it does something to you. I saw both sides do things to civilians that I hope never to see again. It changed my boys to see what horrors men can do to one another. When the summer offensive started and we did get sent up, everybody in my unit managed to stay on this side of the ground for nearly two weeks—until in the middle of an assault, I sent Moretti back behind the lines to fetch something for me. I meant to save him, to get him out of harm's way. He got ten yards before a Kraut machine gun opened fire and cut him clean in two. He was still alive when I got to him, but there wasn't enough of him left to carry on with. He was screaming like a banshee. I unholstered my sidearm and put a bullet in his head.

"That affected the boys pretty bad. I didn't have time to ponder on it, though, what with the tanks coming and all."

His voice trailed off and his gaze wandered away from the window to a blank space on the wall. Alafair didn't think he was looking at anything in this world.

"We lasted another couple of hours. The Germans started shelling our position with one of those big guns of theirs, and the next thing I knew, I was waking up in a field hospital with a cracked head. I never saw any of my unit again, though I heard some of them made it out.

"After the docs released me, I was temporarily assigned to a unit of English boys from Newcastle. They needed a sharp-shooter, and I volunteered. They were just youngsters. England had been fighting a lot longer than we had. I reckon the older boys were all dead by that time. I was with the Tommys for some weeks. It was funny the way them boys looked at me. Like they half expected me to have spurs on my boots and six-shooters strapped to my hip. They were funny, though. Stupid, but funny. The way they talked made me laugh—that is, when I could get a handle on what they were saying at all.

"Their officer was Lieutenant Nigel Anderson. He called himself a 'Leff-tenant.' He was about the same age as me but you'd have thought he was eighty by the way he carried himself.

I can't say we got to be friends. Nobody who had been in the trenches any length of time made friends. But we did have a bond. He knew what had happened to my unit. We never said it to each other, but we both were bound and determined to keep them English boys alive as long as we could. Neither of us thought there was much possibility of any of us getting out of that ditch, but we did our damnedest. I admired that 'Lefftenant' for the way he cared about his troops. He didn't have a high opinion of his generals. But he did his duty, even when some order came down that was downright suicide. That happened with some regularity. Orders would come down to go over the top at such-and-such a day and some hour or the other, and Anderson would go off by himself and cuss like the devil. He used words I'd never heard, but I found them a pretty handy way to supplement my own vocabulary. He'd ask me to creep out of the trench and shoot as many Huns as I could before X-hour. I'd find me a likely spot, up in a tree or somewhere different than I'd used before.

"After what happened with Moretti, with my own boys, I felt nothing. I killed people. I filled my clips and I killed people's sons and husbands and brothers and never felt a thing. When the first cartridge box was empty, I put it in my kit bag and started on the second.

"I was with Anderson's sergeant major, a career soldier named Connor, hard as nails. We were assessing the Germans' strength and getting the lay of the land before the next assault. With all the shelling on both sides, you never could tell from day to day what the ground was like. It was a nice day. I remember that because it was so unusual. Most of the time it never did anything but rain. Sergeant Major Connor was maybe ten yards ahead of me. I was crawling along on my belly in the brush, getting all filthy and scratched but glad to be out of that stinking trench, when Connor ran across a German soldier who took off from his hidey-hole like a quail flushed out of the brush. He ran right toward me, so I tackled him and brought him down. He was hollering some gibberish and I stood up and unslung my rifle.

He was probably scouting our position just like we were doing to him. I had every intention of finishing him off until he flipped over and looked up at me.

"He couldn't have been more than twelve years old. He was crying like a baby and his face was all streaked where the tears had washed away the dirt. He was blue-eyed and his hair was the color of cotton, but all of a sudden his face changed and I was looking down at Private Moretti. I nearly passed out. Sergeant Connor had got to us by then. Judging from the way Connor gaped at me, I must have looked mighty strange. He didn't say anything, but he drew his sidearm. He aimed to finish the boy off if I wasn't going to do it. I grabbed the young'un up by the collar and said I was taking him back to Anderson for interrogation.

"That night when I cleaned my weapon I found one bullet still in the chamber. It was the last one from the second cartridge box. It should have ended up in that child's head."

Gee Dub turned around. Alafair's eyes were brimming and Shaw looked like he had been punched. Gee Dub was relieved not to see an expression of revulsion on either face. He reached into his breast pocket and held up the cartridge between his thumb and forefinger.

"But I kept it instead. The boy was the first German I could have killed, but didn't. I don't know what Connor told Anderson later. The next morning before the assault, Anderson shook my hand and said 'thank you very much' and shipped me back to the Americans. The war ended three days later. I don't know what became of Anderson or his Newcastle lads.

"I think of Moretti a lot. I talk to him, too. He helps me make sense of things sometimes. Moretti kept me from killing the German boy. He kept me from killing Dan Johnson, too. I saw Holly come out of Johnson's house. She was so sad, so wounded. I waited until she was out of sight. I didn't have it in mind to kill him when I went up the porch steps, but he took one look at me and took off. He didn't even know who I was. Guilty conscience, I guess. All of a sudden I was on war footing, back in France. I got him by the hair before he could get away and took him down. I must have looked like a madman, because he started bawling and I swear he wet himself. I straddled him and grabbed for my sidearm. I'd have shot him between the eyes, but I had forgot I wasn't armed. Besides, he was crying. He was pathetic. That's when instead of Dan Johnson, I saw Moretti, all blown up, telling me he didn't want to die. But when I pulled him to his feet, he was Johnson again. I was still wound up. I punched him in the face a couple of times and he ran back into the house. Then I left to find Holly. Me and Dan Johnson never exchanged a word."

Chapter Thirty-three

Alafair and Grace accompanied Gee Dub when he went into town to see Holly off on her long trip back to Maine. Holly took her leave of Alice and little Linda at their house and rode to the train station in Alafair's buggy with Grace on her lap and Gee Dub following behind on his chestnut mare, Penny. Alafair said farewell at the station, wishing Holly a pleasant journey and a pleasant life and loading her down with so many cans and jars and bags of homemade food that Holly thought she might get all the way back to Maine before she had to spend a dime to eat. Grace cried a little when she said her good-byes, which made Holly feel a combination of regret and gratification. She didn't like to see her young friend unhappy, but it was nice that someone besides Gee Dub cared that she was leaving. She expected the rest of the Tuckers would be glad to see the back of her.

If that was how Alafair felt about Holly's departure, she did not show it. "Well, Grace-pie, let's you and me run some errands while we're in town and let these two young'uns have some time on their own before they have to part forever."

She clucked at the horse and turned the buggy back toward the main street, leaving Holly and Gee Dub alone on the platform.

Once they were out of sight, Gee Dub said, "You expect Mama is right?"

A gust of wind tugged at Holly's hat and she put her hand on her crown to keep it in place. "About what?"

"That we are parting forever."

A smile lifted the corners of her mouth and she shrugged. "There's no way of telling what the future will bring, is there?"

"I reckon not." He led her to the long bench by the station wall and they sat down side by side.

She reached into one of the food baskets that Alafair had given her and lifted out a small pan covered by a kitchen cloth. "I made this for you."

Gee Dub recognized his mother's pan. "You made me something?"

"I did. Back in Maine, in blueberry season, in the summer when they are ripe on the bush, Mama and me would come home with peck baskets full of big fat berries that dripped juice and dyed everything they touched. My mother would put up quarts and make pies, and dry some berries to last the winter, but my favorite thing was when she'd make a blueberry buckle. It's just a plain white cake with berries in it and a sugar topping, but I love it. This one doesn't have blueberries, but your mother let me use some of her canned blackberries. It isn't quite the same, but I think you'll like it. Your mama said something to me that made me want to make it for you. She said that when you cook for someone you love, it transfers right into the food."

He looked up from the pan in his lap, taken aback.

"Did you tell anyone what happened after we left Council Hill?" Holly didn't look at him when she asked the question.

"No."

"Why not? It would have given you an alibi for that night."

"I might have, if it had come to it. I didn't have to, as it turns out."

"I did tell Sheriff Tucker, you know. Not everything, but enough that he figured it out, and I'm sure he told Mr. Meriwether. You never had to worry about my reputation, Gee Dub. It is not like anyone thought I was a pillar of virtue, anyway."

Gee Dub laughed at that. "Who is? There is not a soul living who isn't full of shame and regret. Or ought to be. But even if I'd tried to weasel my way out of trouble by spilling my guts, it wouldn't have done any good, anyway. There was still that unaccounted time between when you left Dan's house and met up with me at the cafe."

"Well, no matter. You're an honorable man and I thank you for all you've done for me, from the minute you spied me walking all miserable across that field to this very minute here."

"I could say the same about you, Holly. I think we helped each other."

He had been so solicitous. Her knight, her guardian angel. It had seemed like ages since Holly had plunked herself down in the middle of that muddy field, at the end of her rope and determined to sit there until something happened or she died. Then Gee Dub Tucker had appeared out of nowhere to save her and bring her back to life. Not that she deserved to be saved. Since the day she left Maine, she kept rushing headlong into a viper's pit of trouble. Since the day he found her in the field, Gee Dub kept reaching in to pull her out. She didn't know why.

She had not meant for anyone to know about the night they reached across the long chasm of despair and found each other. She had told him about her nightmare of a father, how her desperation to escape her pain had led her off a cliff and into Dan Johnson's arms. Gee Dub had listened quietly and did not judge her. Then he told her about France.

They had comforted one another that night. Maybe they had even rescued one another. But they both knew that was all it would be. Holly could go back to Maine now. Gee Dub... well, who knew what he would do? But at least he might have a chance to live.

"I don't expect we'll ever see one another again," she told him. "But it's all right. I'm not sorry about anything."

He smiled. "Me neither."

Chapter Thirty-four

Grace was most unhappy that she wouldn't be allowed to wait for the train, so Alafair took her to the Boynton Mercantile and let her pick out a licorice stick to suck on while her mother shopped for thread. Afterwards, they went to the office of the McCoy Land and Title Company to say hello to Martha, then walked the two blocks down Second Street to visit Alice and play with Linda for half an hour. They could have stayed at Alice's house until after the train to Muskogee left Boynton with Holly Thornberry on it and Gee Dub was free to start his life again. But Alafair had a task that she wanted to complete while she was in town.

She pried Grace away from Linda and together they walked back downtown and to the jailhouse. Scott Tucker took his feet off the desk and sat up when the door opened. A wary expression passed over his face when he recognized his visitors.

"Hello, Miss Grace," he greeted, before Alafair could say something to complicate his day. "What brings you to town?"

Grace gave him a grin. Her new teeth were halfway sprouted by now. She was going to have the same wide, toothy smile as the rest of her siblings. "Mama and me and Gee Dub come to take Holly to the train. She's going home to Maine, and that's a long way away. She's going to go to work for her uncle. She said she'd write to me."

"Is that right?" Scott picked up the girl and set her on his knee. Grace was not quite seven, but half her body seemed to be legs. Scott didn't think she'd be sitting on his lap much longer.

Alafair took a seat in one of the bentwood chairs in front of Scott's desk. "Scott, do you still have Harvey Stump's photo, the one that Dan Johnson glued to his own identification card? Can I look at it again?"

Scott had not expected that. He blinked at her. "I suppose you can. What do you want to see it for?"

"I was just thinking about him. From everything I hear, poor old Harvey was a kind and helpful fellow who just had the real bad luck to cross paths with Dan Johnson."

Scott lifted Grace off his lap and stood up to rummage through his file cabinet and retrieve the little photograph of Harvey Stump. He handed it to Alafair.

Harvey looked as young as he was, a little bit surprised to find himself dressed in an Army uniform and sitting in front of a camera. Most of his dark hair had been shaved off except for a bit of unruly frizz on top. He was looking straight at her, his clear pale eyes innocent of his future. The photo had been removed from Dan Johnson's military ID card and clipped to a piece of paper upon which Scott had written the scant known facts of Harvey's life. "Age 20, height 5'10", weight approximately 145 lbs. Parents Sidney and Carlotta Stump, deceased. No siblings. No known relations." A few words about his service were scribbled at the bottom. Harvey had been at Château-Thierry. Alafair wondered if he and Gee Dub had been stationed anywhere near one another.

Grace put an arm over her mother's shoulder and leaned in for a good look at the picture. "Who is that, Ma?"

"That's a poor boy who has gone to his reward, sugar." For an instant Alafair thought she might cry. No one missed Harvey Stump. No one even cared that his young life had been cut short. If Harvey hadn't died of influenza would he have made it home and started a new life, perhaps found a nice girl and married, had children of his own?

She looked up at Scott. "No kinfolks at all have come forward?"

He shook his head. "His mother came over on the boat from Italy all by herself maybe thirty years ago. His daddy was an orphan."

"What's going to happen to all that money Harvey's folks left him?"

Scott shrugged. "It'll end up going to the state of Oklahoma, I reckon."

"Maybe he has kin still living in Italy."

He smiled at her hopeful expression. "Maybe."

"Until y'all find out if that's so, I was thinking that it's a shame that he's lying out there in a pauper's grave without even a marker to show that he ever lived. I talked to Shaw last night and if you think it would be all right, we'd like to pay to have a stone put on his grave."

"I think that Harvey would like that a lot."

Alafair's Recipes

Cornmeal Mush

Makes enough for 4-6 servings

4 cups water
1 tablespoons salt
about 1½ cups yellow cornmeal.

Bring the water to a boil, add salt. Then add cornmeal slowly to boiling water, stirring constantly, until it reaches desired consistency.

Alafair would not have measured the ingredients. She would have brought a pint or two of water to a boil, added a little salt, then taken a handful of cornmeal in one hand and a wooden spoon in the other and drizzled the cornmeal into the water while stirring constantly.

When one handful of meal is gone, scoop another out of the cornmeal bag and drizzle it in the same way, over and over until the mush has thickened enough for the spoon to stand in it. Lower the heat and cook and stir a bit longer until the mush begins to bubble. Be careful. The popping bubbles of cornmeal will burn! This can be eaten like a hot cereal with milk, butter, and syrup or sugar. Or as a hot side dish with gravy or butter, like rice or potatoes.

The most common way to eat cornmeal mush is to cook as above, then pour the hot mush into a loaf pan. When it is cold, slice it, dip each piece in flour and fry it in a little oil or butter, turning to brown both sides.* Alafair would have fried her mush in homemade lard, or perhaps bacon drippings. Serve hot with butter and syrup or sorghum.

*The author's mother never served mush any way but fried.

Indian Pudding

This is a dish which everyone's mother makes her own way. The following basic recipe is not as good as your mother's, but it'll give you an idea. Some people like to add raisins to the batter before baking.

1 cup cornmeal	1 cup minced fat or butter
1 cup light molasses	2 cups cold milk
4 cups whole milk	Salt to taste
1 heaping tablespoon spice	
(ginger, cinnamon, and/or nutmeg, as desired)	

Preheat oven to 350° F. Add the molasses to the cornmeal and beat well together. Add the cornmeal-molasses mix to the quart of boiling milk, along with salt and the desired spices. Add a cup full of minced suet or a piece of butter the size of an egg.

Butter a baking pan and pour in the pudding. Let it stand until thick. Before placing the pan into the oven, pour a pint of cold milk over it, but do not stir. Bake three hours. Serve warm with syrup, cream, or ice cream.

Blueberry Buckle

4-6 servings

Maine is famous for its blueberries, and this delicate cake is a great way to use some of the juicy, fresh berries just picked off of the bush. Since blueberries do not grow wild in Oklahoma, Holly had to use the berries Alafair had on hand. Blackberries grow wild in the eastern part of Oklahoma, so Alafair would have had several jars on hand which she would have canned the previous summer. Holly's cake would not turn out the same as if she had used blueberries, but it would still be delicious. If using canned fruit, be sure to drain and rinse before adding the fruit to the batter.

Cake:

¼ cup butter, softened	¾ cup sugar
1 egg	2 cups all-purpose flour
2 teaspoons baking powder	¼ teaspoon salt
½ cup milk	2 cups fresh blueberries

Topping:

⅔ cup sugar	½ cup all-purpose flour
½ teaspoon ground cinnamon	⅓ cup cold butter, diced

The cake: Cream the butter and sugar together until light and fluffy. Beat in egg. In a separate bowl, sift together the flour, baking powder, and salt and add to creamed mixture alternately with milk. Beat well after each addition. Fold in the fruit and pour the batter into a greased 9 by 9-inch pan.

The topping: Combine the sugar, flour, and cinnamon in a bowl, then rub in the butter with your fingers until the mixture is crumbly. Sprinkle over the cake batter in the pan.

Bake at 375° for 40-45 minutes or until a toothpick inserted near the center comes out clean.

Red Eye Gravy

After frying several slices of country ham in butter, deglaze the skillet (a cast iron skillet is best) with a cup of strong black coffee. Use a spatula to loosen the meat bits that have stuck to the bottom of the pan. Add a cup of water and simmer the gravy until it has reduced by half. After the gravy is poured into a dish or gravy boat, the coffee and meat bits will sink to the bottom and the drippings will rise to the top. Long ago, some clever wag decided that the dark coffee under the clear grease looks like a human eye looking up from the bowl. Yum! Give it a stir before spooning the gravy onto your rice or potatoes.

Crawdads

Crayfish, or crawdads, as they are known in Alafair's part of the world, are very common in Oklahoma. These relatives of lobsters can be found in deep ditches close to lakes, ponds and creeks. Shallow, muddy areas are the best place to catch them. They can be caught by hand if you're quick, or in a trap baited with bacon or fish bits. Using a garden rake with chicken wire wrapped around the tines to drag the bottom of the shallows and sift through the mud works well at catching them. In Cherokee folklore, the crawdads are called "the builders of land" and are responsible for all the dry land in the world. Burrowing crawdads build up mud towers around their holes, and the Cherokees say that they have been piling up dry land since the creation of the Earth.

Bring a large pot of water to a boil, add vegetables (onions, potatoes) and seasonings if you wish (lemon juice, Cajun seasonings), but this is not mandatory. While waiting for the water to boil, rinse the crawdads in clean water. Some people add salt to the rinsing water to purge the crawdads before cooking.

When the water boils, drop the crawdads in and boil for about five minutes, until the shells turn bright red. Turn off the fire and steep the crawdads for 15-20 minutes.

Drain and serve with butter, lemon juice, or whatever dipping sauce you like. A good Southern crawdad boil often includes sausages. Great with corn on the cob, too.

How to eat a crawdad: grab the crawdad at the tail joint and break it in half with a twisting motion. Peel the shell from the tail just as you would peel a shrimp and tug out the luscious tail meat. A real aficionado will also suck the juice from the crawdad's head.

Preserves

If you grow most of your own food, you don't let all of that labor or any of your produce go to waste. Late in summer, farmers would place several big ripe watermelons in a tin tub filled with water and family members would sit on the porch of a sultry evening and enjoy a big slice of cool melon (as well as have a seed-spitting contest). This would leave lots of watermelon rind, which one could either feed to the pigs or use to make the most mouthwatering rind preserves to eat all year. A large truck garden with many tomato plants could yield too many tomatoes to eat fresh, so the enterprising housewife would often pull green tomatoes from the vines and preserve them in relish. The following recipes are from Miz Goggie Vincent, and passed on to the author by Miz Vincent's great-grandson, Dr. Edmund Stump. Dr. Stump's handwritten instructions for watermelon rind preserves are reproduced on the next page.

from Goggie Vincent.

Watermelon Rind (is good with Turkey, gravy, mashed potatoes, dried corn, cranberry sauce, hot rolls, fruit cups, and plum pudding.)

1 (one) eaten Watermelon (leave a big juicy boarder of red)

Cut rind in chunks. □□□ Peel. Soak in salt water overnight.
(5 tsp. salt in enough water to cover)

Boil the soaked stuff in alum water until easily pierced
with fork.   (alum size of marble.)

Drain in colander.

Boil in: (since you can't fish the one (1) in.) (footnote: May need 2 or 3 "goes" of syrup]

2½ cups SUGAR
1 cups vinegar (or ½ cup water plus ½ cup vinegar)
Cinnamon bark and ½ dozen cloves (in small mesh bag). and near
the time : 10 to 15 minutes boiling time 10 to 15 minutes.

Put 2 cloves AND 1 piece Cinnamon bark

into each jar :

add rind :

and pour boiling syrup over, in pint jars or smaller (if desired)

Store for at least Two weeks.

Eat and Enjoy.

Watermelon Rind Preserves

Makes about 8 pints,
depending on the size of the watermelon

Cut the rind of one watermelon into chunks. Peel. Soak in salt water overnight. (5 tsp salt in enough water to cover)

Boil in alum water until easily pierced with a fork (alum the size of a marble).

Drain in colander.

Boil rind for 10-15 minutes in:

   2 ½ cups sugar

   1 cup vinegar (or ½ cup water and ½ cup vinegar)

   1 piece cinnamon bark and ½ dozen cloves wrapped in
      a small mesh bag

   (Footnote: may need 2 or 3 "goes" of syrup)

Put 2 cloves and 1 piece cinnamon bark in each sterilized 1 pint jar (or smaller jar if desired).

Add rind and pour boiling syrup over.

Seal jars and store for at least two weeks. Eat and enjoy.

Green Tomato Relish
Makes about 14 pints

One peck* of green tomatoes (ground)
1/2 cup of salt

Let stand overnight in a crock or enamel pot. Drain the liquid in the morning (drain well).
Add large head of cabbage (ground).
Boil in two quarts of mild vinegar for ½ hour.
Add:
    6 large ground onions
    3 red and 3 green sweet peppers (ground)
    10 cups of sugar
    2 tbsp mustard seed
    2 tbsp celery seed
    1 tbsp ground cinnamon or cloves (or both)
Cook all for 20-30 minutes, stirring occasionally. Drain well after cooking.

* One peck tomatoes = @ 10 pounds

To see more Poisoned Pen Press titles:

Visit our website: poisonedpenpress.com/
Request a digital catalog: info@poisonedpenpress.com